PROWLING THEIR MATE

AMELIA SHAW
TAMSIN BAKER

TYLER

1

No... Not her.

Can't do it... Been there.

Done that.

Nope.

I swung away from the dance floor to face the mirrored wall behind the bar and slumped on the stool.

Damn it. Not an attractive woman in sight. Again.

My twin brother was off in some dark corner with a blonde chick who wore too much makeup and clothes so tight she must have painted them on before she left home. I shuddered.

Not my type. Not at all.

"What's up with you?" a familiar female voice asked as she sidled up next to me.

I rolled my eyes at my sister, Renee. *Great. Just what I need.*

I forced my hunched posture to attention, straightening my spine and rolling back my sagging shoulders. "Nothing, sis. What's up with you?"

I reached for my beer and plastered a smile on my face, trying my best not to look like my world was a desolate place to inhabit.

Which, nowadays, it was.

My gorgeous sister stared back at me, her brows lowered in a disapproving frown.

Renee completed the family trifecta of hair color. I had our father's dark brown locks, Brandon was blond like our mother, which, of course, had somehow left Renee with an amazing head of red hair.

"You look depressed—again—and I'm sick of seeing that, Tyler. What the hell is wrong with you?"

Renee crossed her arms and glared at me with the heated gaze that only a redhead could get away with. The look made me flinch and I took a long drink of my frothy, cold beer.

She was right. But I hated having to deal with her when my mind was in the miserable space it was occupying tonight. She was too hard to ignore and she read me far too accurately. How could I tell her the truth?

"I've just had a rough week at work, sis. Nothing more."

She punched me in the arm, hard, knocking me off balance. I grabbed the edge of the bar to steady myself as pain rippled across my upper right chest and I rocked on the barstool.

"Ow!" I glared at her and rubbed the sore spot with my free hand. She really could pack a punch, this woman. I was kinda proud. Brandon and I had taught Renee to fight from a young age and no one had ever taken advantage of her, to my knowledge.

I glared right back. "Hey, sis! You're not supposed to bite the hand that feeds you. We taught you to fight so you could punch out other guys, not us."

"Tell me the truth!" she demanded, obviously refusing to be dissuaded from her path. Her path being, to find out what was bugging me.

She stomped her foot and placed both hands on her hips. *What a freaking princess!*

I rolled my eyes again and inhaled sharply through my nose. I knew she wouldn't give up until I answered.

"I'm lonely, okay?" I finally admitted. "Work's great, the family's fine, but I'm fucking sick of chasing random and meaningless tail."

Renee's whole posture relaxed and she slid onto the stool next to me. "Whiskey, neat," she called to the bartender and placed her hand on my leg, patting my thigh. "You'll find her soon. I know you will."

I grunted and lifted my beer again. I had no doubt I'd find my mate one day, but when? I'd already waited long enough and I was losing patience.

"Yeah, but when? I'm damn sick of waiting. Dad told us that we have no control over our destiny, and that Fate will take care of everything, but seriously? I'm fucking thirty-two. I've been dating for fifteen years already and I'm done. I want a family. I'm ready for that. More than ready."

I clenched my hand into a fist, so tight that pain shot up my fingers and through my palm.

"Hey, Ty. I'm heading back to the house. You comin'?"

Brandon, my fraternal twin, thumped me on the back and I grimaced. What? He wanted me to play third wheel again to whatever stray woman he'd come across this week?

"No, thanks. Nae will give me a ride." I looked at our sister to confirm, and she nodded. I unclenched my throbbing fingers and tried to ignore how uncomfortable I was at this point of my life.

Brandon took off with the blonde Barbie doll.

Renee sighed as she watched Brandon leave and downed her whiskey with a quick flick of her wrist and a practiced swallow. "It doesn't look like big brother is going to be lonely tonight."

She was right, but she was also wrong. I knew how it felt to fill your cold nights with random women, and while it might satisfy a physical craving, it did not necessarily cure the loneliness. One-night stands were not the way to happiness. At least, not for me. If anything, they only accentuated the lack of love in my life.

I shook my head and called for another drink. "Nope, not Brandon. Although at the rate he's going, we're gonna have to move soon, so he'll have fresh pickings to choose from."

Renee laughed and elbowed me in the side. "Hey, glass houses, brother of mine. It wasn't that long ago you were dragging some woman home every other night, too."

I know. You don't have to remind me.

I stared blankly at the countertop and rolled my empty glass slowly between my hands. It was true. I'd practiced the art of wooing and screwing, just like Brandon. Why not? I'd been young and had been told that I had to wait until Fate deemed it time to send the right woman my way.

I'd figured I might as well go out looking and hasten the process along. But it'd been almost fifteen years since my first girlfriend and I was tired of waiting. I wanted to find my forever *now*. The woman I was meant to love, who was created to be with me.

My fated mate.

Renee turned to me. "What if you have to wait until Brandon's ready, too?"

Frustration clawed through my heart. *God, no. Please.*

I groaned and reached for the newly poured beer the bartender placed in front of me. That was my worst fear—that Fate would wait until both of us were ready to settle down.

"Honestly, Nae? Then I'm fucked. He doesn't ever look like wanting to settle down."

My family were shifters, mountain lion shape-shifters, to be exact. We all lived in a small town at the base of the Canadian Rockies.

My dad had pulled Brandon and me aside when we were nearly ten, to explain about the birds and the bees. The only difference in the speech we got instead of the "normal" one came at the end of the talk, when our dad explained our future.

"You two are a perfect pair. Perfect compliments to each other in physical appearance and personality."

We'd nodded, not really knowing what that meant. I remember waiting for the signal to go back to play. That's when Dad hit us with the line that would change our lives forever.

"And that means that, when the time comes, you will mate with a single female. Together."

"*What!*" We boys had glared at each other and pouted. Though twins, we rarely shared anything. If we fought over a bike, how would we possibly be able to share a mate?

Our father had smiled and touched us both on the cheek. *"It'll be fine."*

Unfortunately, it was not fine. We were thirty-two years old and only one of us was ready for our forever woman. If I had to share her with Brandon, then so be it. I would learn how to deal with that. But where was she?

I glanced over at my baby sister. "I can't imagine finding a woman that we're both gonna like. Brandon's always gone for tall blondes."

"And you've always gone for the short brunettes," Renee finished for me. "We know, Ty."

My head began to spin and I finished the rest of my drink, embracing the wooziness. It was a nice reprieve from the usual cold feeling in my gut that had become more pronounced recently.

"You know, I think I'll walk home, Nae."

Renee jumped to her feet and touched my arm gently. "No, I'll drive you."

I groaned and shook my head. "Thanks, but I'll be fine. It's only fifteen minutes. That'll give Brandon a chance to finish with the blonde."

The last thing I wanted to do was walk in on *that* scene.

Renee chuckled and squeezed my arm tight, the same way she had when I was younger and my first dog had been hit by a car. With love and compassion. "Goodnight, bro."

I stumbled forward and pulled my sister into my body for a one-armed hug. She was the best, she really was.

"Night, sis."

I walked out into the cold night air and took a deep breath. My mountain lion wanted to run, but the last time I'd shifted while drunk, I'd woken up locked in a zoo cage. My mother would kill me if that ever happened again.

I shook my head and laughed, imagining that conversation. My mother was not one to mince her words.

So, instead of shifting and running through the forest like I desired, I began the lonely walk back to the house I shared with my twin.

LAURA

2

I was going to kill my stupid sister if it was the last thing I ever did. I put my cell on speaker and dialed Belle's number for the fifth time, growling at the phone. "Where the hell are you?"

Belle's phone finally picked up and I heard a familiar giggling down the line. "H'lo?"

Oh, thank God!

"Belle! Where are you?"

Belle giggled again and I rolled my eyes heavenward.

A little help, please!

"Belle, you have to be at that University Open House tomorrow or you won't be accepted."

Belle laughed as though that was the greatest joke she'd ever heard, and slurred into the phone.

"I wasss...at the li'l bar on the corner and now I'm goin' home with Brandon..."

I grabbed my keys and headed out the front door.

Calm. I needed to stay calm.

"That's great, hon. Can you ask him to give you his address and I'll come pick you up in a little while?" I made my voice as light and friendly as possible, hoping to convince my horny little sister to come home early.

"It's 48 Cabin Creek Drive," came a husky reply from a male voice. Presumably the aforementioned Brandon.

I shivered. His voice was like salted caramel over vanilla ice cream. So smooth and decadent, my knees almost buckled beneath me.

Damn it... What the hell was that?

I shook myself as I walked down the path, wrenched open my car door, and jumped in. Cabin Creek Drive wasn't far.

"Don't leave. I'll be there soon to collect you."

I put my car into gear and pulled out into the empty road. This was the last thing I wanted to be doing on a Friday night, chasing down Belle... again. But hey, what else was there for me to do tonight?

Wasn't like I had a life of my own or anything...

Twenty-two minutes later, I pulled up outside a beautiful double-story house. It was at the end of a block of homes at the edge of the residential estate bordering the forest at the base of the Rocky Mountains.

My eyes widened at the size of the place. "Wow."

I stepped out of the car and looked up at the well-maintained home and lawn lit by attractive landscape lighting.

Who was this guy? A luxury house builder? An architect?

"Can I help you?"

I spun around and fell back against the car as a force I didn't recognize almost knocked me off my feet.

The man standing in front of me had a face that looked like it'd been carved by angels. Dark eyes that, even at a distance, burned with heat. His short, dark hair was styled casually and his body looked strong and wiry.

I swallowed against the lump that rose in my throat and felt an intense pull in my lower belly. My primitive side that I didn't like to admit was even a part of me, responded to the attraction of this exceptionally hot-looking male.

"Uh, yes. Hopefully you can." I cleared my throat and staggered forward on legs that were shaking. I must have looked drunk.

"You all right?" the man asked. He stepped forward and grabbed my bare elbow.

I gasped as sparks flew up my arm and tingled all the way to my core. My heart thumped against my ribs and I bit back a moan.

I'd never felt anything like it before.

"*Fuck!*" The gorgeous guy growled, letting go of me as though he'd been burned. Had he felt that electric zap, too?

He backed up so quickly I almost fell forward into the front hedge that bordered the property.

He continued to growl with weird, panting noises, sounding much like a large and very predatory cat.

His eyes flickered from their dark brown color to a strange, tawny yellow. I blinked, but the color change was still there. Was there something wrong with him, or was the dim light playing games with my eyesight?

I looked at him, hard... and saw it again. Brown to tawny and back to brown. What the hell was this guy on?

"What's wrong with you?" he demanded roughly, as though *I* were the one behaving oddly.

I straightened up and glared at him. This man was a stranger and I was here to get my sister. *Get your head on straight.*

"Nothing is wrong with me." I flicked my hair back and squared my shoulders. "I'm here to pick up Belle. She told me she'd be here."

The man nodded with jerky motions, still breathing like he'd run a marathon, and gestured for me to follow.

"She's probably inside. With my brother."

His voice had dropped a couple of octaves and, as he strode up the steps to the house and unlocked the front door, I got a great view of his tight ass.

Stop perving on him, stupid! When has a man like that ever looked at you?

I pulled my short-sleeve pink cardigan tighter around my overly generous breasts and muffin top resting on the waistband of my jeans. It was a shame it wasn't fall, when I would likely be wrapped in my winter puffy jacket to hide the evidence of my love of all things carbs.

"In here!" a guy called out, and I shivered as the voice from the phone rang through the air.

His voice was like chocolate—smooth, hot, and melted.

And he likes girls like Belle. Tiny, blonde... and a bit on the silly side.

Heat seared my cheeks as I followed behind the dark-haired man who was still looking like he wasn't comfortable in his own skin.

I walked down the hallway and into a massive kitchen and living space. Parquet floors and modern, expensive-looking furniture featured in what was a relatively spotless and very impressive home.

Wow. Two men really live here? Maybe they're gay and I just made an idiot of myself.

"She's in the bathroom."

I dragged my eyes away from the garden and forest view out the floor-to-ceiling windows and looked toward the melted chocolate voice.

Oh my God!

The same force that hit me outside pounded into my chest and sent me stumbling against the marble counter. My heart raced against my ribs as blood flowed through my body at a lightning-fast pace.

What the heck was wrong with me? Sweat broke out along my neckline and if I didn't know better, I'd think I was having a heart attack.

"What the hell is going on?" I gasped the words out loud without meaning to, clutching at my chest.

The two men shared a look and some form of silent communication passed between them. Maybe they really were a couple. Stupid Belle had gone home with a gay guy, or at least a bisexual one.

The first guy that I'd met outside turned to face me, his hands gripping the chair next to him so tightly his knuckles glowed white.

"I'm Tyler and this is my twin brother, Brandon."

Oh, thank God they're not gay.

Didn't think my gaydar was that far off!

I looked between the two men, who could have easily graced the front cover of any men's health or fashion magazine. They were almost carbon copies of each other in facial features, yet with totally opposite coloring. "Obviously, you're not identical."

The men chuckled and glanced at each other again. I noted that Tyler was slightly smaller in build and height than Brandon, though not by much.

"No, we're not identical," Tyler said. "What's your name?"

I straightened and folded my arms across my chest, heat flushing up my neck. The things they must be thinking... I was always a disappointment to anyone who met Belle first.

"I'm Laura." *The big, fat, nerdy sister.*

Both men repeated my name and made strange, purring noises in their throats.

I frowned at them. "What is with that noise?"

Tyler ignored my question. Instead, he looked at his brother and gestured toward me. "Go shake her hand."

Brandon stared at Tyler dumbly, but moved forward anyway.

"Hello." He walked within an arms-length of me and extended his hand.

I stared at the massive palm and that odd shiver caressed my spine again.

I reached out and our skin connected.

"Holy shit!" Brandon jumped back in a similar way that Tyler had earlier, and heat pooled in my lower belly. I rubbed my hand along my jeans, the zinging within my skin lasting just as long as when I'd touched Tyler.

Heat stole across my cheeks as the warmth turned into a deep, arousing throb right at the center of my being. I opened my mouth to ask another question when an unpleasant noise broke through my concentration on the two men.

It sounded like someone throwing up.

I cleared my throat. "Is that my sister?" I lifted my chin toward the sound of vomiting.

Brandon nodded and crossed his arms over his massive chest. A few buttons had been popped and I got a good view of golden skin and blond, curly chest hair.

Had my sister been the one to unbutton that shirt, or had Brandon done it himself?

I inhaled sharply and ignored the strange looks I was getting from the men. I strode forward and a deep twinge of sadness tugged at my heart when both of them moved rapidly out of my way.

Was I that repulsive that they couldn't bear to touch me again? Or did I look like I had something contagious?

I tried to push aside my feelings of rejection and focused on my little sister.

"Belle?" I called out as I knocked on the partially open wooden door and sighed when it opened fully. My shoulders sagged in defeat at the sight before me.

Seriously?

My beautiful sister was slumped on the bathroom floor, vomit covering her half-exposed tiny, perky breasts.

I whirled around to face the man who'd brought her home, lashing him with my anger.

"Do I have to worry about a morning after pill? Or didn't you quite get that far?"

Brandon's face contorted and turned bright red. "Are you kidding me? You think I'd fuck a vomiting, half-conscious woman?"

He looked truly perturbed by the idea, his face twisting into a grotesque mask.

I turned away to hide my relief. The man might swear like a sailor, but I couldn't fault his moral compass on this one.

"Excuse me."

I stepped into the bathroom and shut the door on the two men.

For fuck's sake, Belle!

I let out a sigh that should have belonged to our mother. But both of our parents were long dead and buried, so Belle was my responsibility and it was time to get my sister cleaned up. *Again.*

Yuck. Not a pleasant task, but I'd certainly dealt with worse when it came to her.

I had to get her home and ready to begin her new life.

Belle was not missing out on this opportunity for future study. I would make sure of it. She needed the chance to reach for everything in life she deserved.

BRANDON

3

My abs were quivering like I'd just run ten miles in marathon time. What the hell was wrong with my body? My heart was pounding, my hands were shaking, and I could swear my balls had never felt so tight.

"Who the hell is she?" I demanded of my brother.

Tyler tightened his grip on the kitchen counter top and growled like the wild animal that was trapped inside both of us.

"Hey. Stop it!" I stepped away from my brother's vibrating figure and opened the fridge, pulling out two cold beers. "What's wrong with you?"

My brother was smaller than I was, in both our human form and our lion. As such, I was usually the more aggressive and dominant of the two of us.

But in this moment, fear pricked my spine. I'd never heard my brother make such a noise before. As if he were teetering on the very edge of control.

"I...can't..." Tyler dropped his head and stretched back, his brown hair beginning to lighten and change into the characteristically golden fur of the Canadian Rockies' mountain lion.

Fuck!

"No! Ty, pull yourself together. Not while we have guests."

Tyler's head shot up, his eyes already changed to tawny yellow and his nose beginning to morph into the face of the lion.

Shit. It was already too late. Tyler's human body was gone and in the midst of the pool of his clothes on the floor stood an enormous mountain lion.

"Go. Quick."

Tyler took off through the house and I raced after him. Watching him go, even in this erratic state, I still felt an incredible lightness of heart as I watched my brother nudge open the unlocked screen door with his head and leap out into the night.

He disappeared into the darkness and I knew he'd be heading into the forest right now. I walked back to the kitchen, picked up Ty's clothes and threw them down the chute that led to the laundry in the basement.

The girls still hadn't come out of the bathroom, so I took a swig of beer, the cold hops relieving some of the dryness in my mouth and throat.

I had asked my brother who the hell she was, but deep down, I already knew.

I think we've found our mate.

I sympathized with my brother. I knew what had caused Tyler's shift, even if he hadn't been able to articulate it.

I had pretty strong control over my lion, and yet the shifter inside me was prowling. Pacing back and forth inside me, along with the wild emotions surging through me.

I hadn't kissed her yet, so I couldn't be sure, but I suddenly began to believe my father may have been telling the truth about our destiny.

Part of me had always hoped our dad was wrong. How could there be just one woman destined for both Tyler and me? Plus I didn't like the idea of having no control over my own life. My own destiny. If we were part of some grand "fated" plan, it didn't mean I had to just fall into line. I did have some say in how I lived my life. I had always been totally against being told what to do and with whom to mate.

Maybe that was one of the reasons I'd hooked up so often—

something contrary deep within me that wanted control over what happened in my life. And with whom.

But the touch of Laura's skin against mine had been nothing short of brilliant.

I ran my hand through my hair and shook my head.

She was nothing like the woman I had imagined as a mate. Nothing like what I normally was attracted to. Physically, she wasn't thin or dressed to impress, and I could see the keen intelligence in her eyes. She wouldn't be easy to talk around to my way of things.

Not at all.

I glanced toward the back door and sighed. Tyler losing control like that wasn't a good thing. I'd learned how to control my lion during my teenage years, letting it rise and fall enough times to truly accept the shifter as part of myself. Tyler hadn't.

He'd fought our natural form every step of the way.

"Brandon?" Laura's smooth, sensual voice called out to me and I turned toward her like so many men before me, responding to the call of a siren.

The hairs on my arms prickled as our gazes met. Damn, she had a beautiful face.

"Can you help me get Belle into my car?"

I nodded and set my drink down on the kitchen table, not trusting myself to speak. I wasn't sure words would come out. So I stayed mute and walked forward, swinging the tiny blonde up into my arms.

I couldn't help the instant comparison of the two sisters that flashed through my mind.

Belle was a Barbie doll. Skinny, pretty, and incredibly common. I'd talked to her for half an hour at most, like I always did before I brought anyone home.

I was a builder, not an architect like my brother, yet I still struggled to engage with airhead women. Dumbing down every sentence while flirting to keep them interested was not my strong suit. I generally ended up bored out of my brain, but at least they usually agreed to come home with me.

For some reason I hated sleeping alone and my sex drive had hit an all-time high recently. It was as if I'd been searching for something... *someone*. If that was on account of *her*, then I hoped she'd be able to handle me.

And Tyler too, if my dad was to be believed.

Laura walked ahead of us, her lush ass swinging seductively in her jeans. Okay, I had to admit it... Laura was pretty sexy. Beautiful, even. Just not in a currently popular way.

She had magnificent green eyes without a hint of makeup distracting from them, and delicious-looking skin. I didn't usually go for overly fleshy women, but she had perfect proportions. Her huge, bouncing breasts were just begging to be exposed to the cool air and I could imagine sucking on them until her nipples were hard peaks begging for more..

Blood flowed straight to my cock, arousal sweeping through me as I imagined what Laura would feel like beneath me.

Perfect, probably.

"Thanks for this," she said, as we walked down the front steps of the porch and along the garden path. When we got to the car, she opened the door for me.

I deposited Belle onto the seat. She was groaning and burping like a baby. She smelled like vomit too. *Great.*

"I'll strap her in."

I stepped back to allow Laura to slide by me and got a whiff of her incredible scent. Honeysuckle and daisies—fresh, earthy, and clean. I wanted to roll in the smell. Close my eyes, and get lost in it.

Fuck... move away now!

That saving grace thought made me stagger away as my lion rose to the surface. There was pressure in my rib cage and a need to fall away into the abyss, allowing my cat to surface. He was calling for his mate, needing to claim Laura as his own.

I pushed my lion down with a struggle, physically clenching my abdominals and exhaling deeply to contain him.

As I watched the woman my lion believed to be *my woman* ready herself to leave, I realized I had to stop her. I couldn't just let her go.

"Where do you live?"

Laura righted Belle up in her seat, kissed her forehead like a mother would, and shut the door. My lion purred happily inside me at the show of maternal instinct within Laura as she moved around to her side of the relatively new car.

Obviously, Laura wasn't a student like Belle.

"Why?" Laura asked, her elegant eyebrow quirking up.

Shit... why, why, why?

"Ah...I'd like to check on Belle tomorrow."

Yes. Good one.

As Laura's mouth turned down, I realized using Belle probably wasn't the best way to stay in touch with the older sister.

"You didn't get her number?"

I shook my head. More than likely I wouldn't have gotten around to asking for it, even if I had bedded her.

"I probably shouldn't help you here—but you know what—who am I to stand in the way of true love?" Her voice dripped with sarcasm and I worked hard not to let the flush spread across my face.

True love. Yeah, right.

"What's your number?" she asked.

I recited my cell number and she pressed several buttons on her phone.

"There. Done."

She gave me a mocking wave and slid into her car before driving away.

Pride blossomed in my chest as my lion rose to the surface once again. She was strong and fiercely protective. Exactly as a mate should be.

I held it together by holding my breath and pressing down on my diaphragm until the car disappeared, then I bolted inside. I had to join my brother and shift too. My skin burned and my groin was on fire.

I stripped as quickly as possible and roared as my body transformed.

A contented rumble bubbled inside my chest as I stretched within my new body then ran out the door as fast as I could. When I reached the lake, I inhaled my twin's scent. Tyler had been here recently.

I needed to track him down. We both needed to spend the night sorting out our own demons, before we approached Laura once again.

Tyler would accept our fate with an open heart. I knew that as surely as I knew my blood was red. My twin had always embraced our father's prediction of our fated mate being out there somewhere, but I had never been sure if it was fact or fiction.

I'd always wondered if our father was just passing down a story, or if it would happen no matter what I did?

If Laura was the one for us, how was she going to be enough for us both? Even when I gave some woman a chance at a semi-relationship, within a couple of nights I was bored stupid. And sexually, they couldn't keep up with my hunger. I would end up frustrated and feeling more alone than ever.

I turned around and took a slower pace back around to the house, my body no longer burning in its need for freedom.

This woman—Laura—was going to change everything.

Instead of peace or happiness, inside me was restless fear, and I hated being helpless against it. My future was full of more waiting. Unfortunately I could think of no other way out of this mess than to see how it went with Laura.

If we developed some sort of ménage mating situation, then I could always keep my one-night stands on the side if I needed to. Couldn't I? I'd be honest with her about it. I would owe her that. But surely, if I was discreet, Laura wouldn't care?

It didn't matter what my father had said, no destiny could be better than the freedom I had now.

And no woman was going to keep me starving when there was a plethora of available females out there.

Tyler

I woke with a terrible hangover, my head pounding and my body aching from the long-overdue run last night. The beers hadn't helped my cause, either.

"For crying out loud." I groaned as I rolled onto my back in bed and squeezed my palms against the sides of my head.

It sounded like someone was ringing a gong in there.

"Morning!" my stupid brother called out as he walked through my bedroom door, already showered and dressed.

"God, Brandon! How are you so fucking chirpy?"

Brandon chuckled and handed me a glass of water with a couple of painkillers.

"Practice."

That'd be right.

I forced myself to sit up, my head spinning faster with the change of altitude.

"Thanks." I swallowed the white pills down with a splash of water, relishing the feel of the cool liquid sliding down my dry throat.

"I'm going to call Laura this morning," he said. "You want in?"

The hairs on my neck prickled and I placed my glass down on the nightstand.

I'd pushed most thoughts of last night from my mind, but Brandon's comment brought it all rushing back.

Was it really possible?

Had we found our mate?

"You were attracted to Laura, too?"

Brandon crossed his meaty arms over his chest, then nodded

once. "Yeah, I think so. I mean, she's not exactly my type..."

I groaned, frustration clawing at my gut. I knew Brandon was gonna say that. "Yeah, I know that. But you feel it too, don't you? She's our mate. Right?"

Brandon dropped his arms down and began to pace. "I always thought our woman would be a shifter."

I nodded slowly, relieved to find my headache was disappearing. "Yeah, but we looked at them all years ago."

And we had. Following our parents' urging, we'd dated most of the female mountain lion shifters and found nothing enthralling about any of them.

We both knew it would be so much easier if our mate had been a shifter too. Someone we didn't have to introduce to... *everything*.

Now, we had to get Laura used to the idea of us both wanting her, and the fact that we turned into animals whenever we wanted to. Not that I'd had much experience with telling non-shifter humans about us, but from what I understood, it wasn't an easy thing for a human to understand... or accept.

And then on top of that, we had to get her to understand the fated mate bond.

"So, what's the plan then?"

I looked up and saw a shadow of confusion cross Brandon's face. He was definitely not one to think through something before he did it.

"What do you mean?" Brandon cocked his head and stopped pacing.

I swung my legs off the bed, not liking the dizzy sensation swirling around my brain. "I mean, how are you planning on getting her to agree to be our mate? She's not going to just move in and accept two of us, is she?"

Brandon frowned, his handsome face wrinkling. "Why not?"

I laughed without mirth and got to my feet. "I'll get dressed. Don't call her before I come out."

Brandon opened his mouth to retort and I let loose a little growl.

Whoa. Those noises are way too easy to make now.

Brandon's eyes widened before he nodded. Then he turned and headed back to the living room.

I showered quickly and dressed, doubt and fear filling my mind.

How the hell were we going to convince an obviously intelligent human woman that she had to love both of us because Fate decreed it? Brandon and I were like night and day. Not many women ever truly liked both of us.

In fact, I was yet to meet a single one.

"Big brother, I presume you have her number?" I called out as I walked into our recently renovated kitchen. Brandon had come out into the world only minutes ahead of me, but that made him the big brother in our family.

Brandon pushed his cell across the countertop. "Yeah. She messaged me Belle's number last night, so I have hers, too."

I was impressed. Smartest thing Brandon had done in years. "So, how are we going to get her to start seeing us?"

Brandon shrugged and I rolled my shoulders back. We needed to be smart about this. The rest of our lives depended on it.

I crossed my arms over my chest, my brain racing with ideas. "We don't even know her last name or where she lives. How 'bout you call to ask about Belle and if you get the opportunity, invite Laura here for dinner... to say thanks."

"Thanks for what, exactly?" Brandon asked, his eyebrows furrowing together.

I clenched my teeth and used all the patience I'd accumulated over the years to deal with my brother. "Thank her for coming here to get her sister, and cleaning her up. Otherwise, you would have had to look after her."

"Oh, yeah. Great idea!" Brandon grabbed at the phone and dialed Laura's number.

"Put it on speaker." I pointed to the cell on the counter and Brandon did, transferring it to loudspeaker and setting the phone down in front of us.

Her cell didn't ring, but instead went straight to voicemail.

"Hello, you've reached Laura Carver."

I shivered as her delicious voice filled the cavernous space.

"This is Dr. Carver. Please leave a message. If this is after regular office hours and your pet is having a medical emergency, please call our emergency service at (555) 333-1200 and we will be paged."

Brandon pressed the red button to end the call and looked up at me slowly, his blue eyes filled with mischief. "She's a... vet?"

A moment of silence passed between us, then we burst out laughing.

Oh my God. Of all the things she could be, it had to be an animal doctor.

"Hope she likes big cats," I said, before chuckling again.

I collapsed onto one of the kitchen stools, holding my aching side with one hand. Just what our family of lion shifters needed—a vet.

"Mom'll be thrilled." Brandon chortled as he walked to the fridge and grabbed the juice.

"She'll be intelligent, too," I mused, pleased by this turn of events. I'd always wanted a mate I could talk to, share concepts with. But with Brandon more impressed by looks than smarts, I'd been worried that our mate would be a little on the less intelligent side.

Like Laura's sister, Belle.

"Yeah," Brandon said, his enthusiasm clearly lacking at this turn of events.

"It'll be fine." I said as reassuringly as I could, then jumped to my feet and headed toward the study. "I'm gonna search the internet for a veterinarian named Laura Carver and see what I find."

Brandon made a grunting noise and I continued on my quest for knowledge about our new mate.

I was an architect and Brandon was a builder.

We were both successful in our own right, and hard-working. But when it came to the brains versus brawn debate, Brandon generally left the thinking and planning side of things to me.

BRANDON

4

I cooked bacon and eggs, shuffling some onto a plate for Tyler in case he was hungry. We were so used to looking after ourselves. What would it be like when a chick moved in?

"I found her!" Tyler cried as he walked back into the kitchen, waving a piece of paper with a triumphant air.

"Where?" I asked. Not that I had a lot of interest at this point. Laura didn't sound like a suitable mate for me. Tyler—yes. Me, not so much.

I brought our breakfast plates to the table, sat down and grabbed my coffee mug.

"Hinton. About thirty minutes away. She works in a small vet clinic there. Maybe one of us could surprise her at work?"

I wasn't sure I should be the one doing the *wooing* in this situation. Tyler was much more impressive on paper than me, and even though he was the less physically imposing of us, he still had a decent body.

"Maybe you should go see her, Ty. I mean, she's obviously pretty clever, and I'm not sure how much she's gonna love me when she remembers that I picked up her sister last night."

Tyler opened his mouth, then shut it quickly.

I could almost hear his thoughts whirling.

It could have been a lot worse.

Hell yes, it could've.

I continued. "Pretty big coincidence, but at least I didn't fuck her."

Tyler frowned and looked down at the address again. What else could be said, really? I'd potentially ruined our chance to be with Laura before we'd even properly gotten to know her.

Tyler surprised me when he glanced up and said, "Yeah, and really... it was probably a good thing last night happened, or we would never have met Laura. She doesn't look like the sort of woman who hangs around bars looking for a date."

The weight I'd been carrying since last night lifted. Maybe I hadn't completely fucked everything up. Yet. "Thanks, Ty."

His observation was a good way of looking at it, and one I hadn't considered.

Tyler picked up his fork and started eating. "Maybe I should get one of Mom's pets and schedule a visit at her clinic?"

I nodded at my brother. "Great idea. Then casually drop into the conversation something about how we both want to mate her for life."

I froze, and blinked in shock at the words that had come out of my mouth.

Well, that sounds heavy.

Tyler gave me a dirty look then dug into the food in front of him.

I gave the look straight back before putting my now-empty plate in the sink. I was restless and edgy, and the food hadn't helped.

I had to get out of here for a bit. "I'm gonna head to the gym."

"You're kidding." Tyler sputtered behind me.

I let my head drop as I thought about what to say. How did Tyler not understand the need for a major workout?

I wasn't sure if being honest was the right thing to do, but I didn't know any other way. When the words came, I turned and threw them at Tyler.

"Ty, I know you've been waiting for this chick forever, but I haven't. You know that. If she really is 'the one' and I have to be mated with her, then so be it. But I'm not going to put my whole life on hold in the meantime."

Tyler pushed himself to his feet, his eyes burning lion-tawny. *Shit,* where had this temper of Ty's come from?

"We need to pursue her... *together.*"

I shook my head and headed toward the bedroom. I didn't want this crap, any of it. How hard was that for my brother to understand?

"Tyler, if you can get her to come over for dinner, I promise I'll be on my best behavior."

I changed into my gym clothes and left the house without a backward glance.

I had a great job, good friends, good health and fitness, and of course, my family. If I had some pre-destined perfect female coming my way, I wasn't going to turn her away, but I certainly wasn't going to go out of my way to get her, either.

Wasn't that Fate's job?

Tyler

I stepped up to the front doorstep of Hinton Veterinary Clinic with an injured dog in my arms. Unfortunate for the dog but very fortunate for me that when I'd called my mom an hour ago to ask about her animals, she'd been about to head to the vet's office. Poor Cotton had been in a fight with a coyote and had come off second best.

I opened the door and stepped into the clinic, the overly sterile smell of surgery assailing my sensitive nose. *Yuck!*

"Can I help you?" a cute woman with freckles and red hair asked from behind the desk.

"Ah, yes." I walked forward, holding Cotton in my arms.

"She got into it with a coyote this morning and has a cut on her front leg, hind leg teeth punctures, and a ripped ear."

Cotton struggled a little and I held the dog firmly against my chest, soothing the warm lump with a soft pat.

"Oh, poor little thing. Please have a seat and I'll have a tech get a room ready for you."

"No! Ah, I'd like to see the vet, Laura, if that's not too much trouble."

The woman stared at me for a moment, then smiled. "Doctor Laura's schedule is packed this morning, but she'll be in to examine Cotton as quickly as possible. We welcome walk-ins but sometimes it takes a bit longer to be seen."

I put as much warmth into my eyes as I could. "Thanks, I appreciate it."

I sat down on one of the uncomfortable, white plastic chairs. My ass was almost numb by the time I was called into a small examination room thirty minutes later.

The back door to the room opened and Laura walked in, her long hair tied up into a bun and wearing a pristine, white lab coat.

"Hello, it's nice to meet... Oh, it's you."

Her green eyes widened and her pupils dilated as she stared at me.

She's attracted to me. Thank God for that.

"I brought Cotton in to see you. She got in a fight this morning."

I placed the injured pup down on the stainless-steel table, patting her soft fur when she whimpered.

"It's okay, pretty girl."

I could feel Laura's eyes boring into me as I concentrated on the dog.

Laura *hmmphed* and stepped forward, running her hands over the dog and connecting with my hand accidentally.

"Oh my God, what is that?" Laura jumped backward. She was shaking her hands out in front of her frantically as though they were burning, which I could relate to. My skin was tingling and I could feel her touch like a permanent tattoo.

"What was *what*?" I asked, not wanting to assume she felt the same tingles running through my body, despite her actions.

Every part of me was awake and alive. I wanted to grab her, hold her close, and kiss those beautiful lips. But instead of following those primitive urges, I withdrew my hands from the dog's fur and clenched them into fists behind my back.

"When... when I touch your skin. I... I can't explain it." Laura was shaking and I hated seeing her like that.

"It's okay, I promise. Would you consider going somewhere with me this afternoon so I can explain?"

Laura stared at me for a moment, then looked down at the dog.

"Step aside for a moment and let me do my job, then I'll give you an answer."

I moved back as Laura stepped forward, running her hands expertly over the shaking dog, examining her from head to tail.

"She needs a shot for the pain and one to prevent a possible infection in her hind leg. I'll put some glue over her leg and ear. The injuries aren't deep enough to need stitches, but she's going to have to wear a cone for a few days to prevent her from re-opening the wounds."

"Thanks." I watched Laura with a sense of pride as she moved about the room. She was efficient, intelligent and capable—everything I'd ever wanted in a mate.

She was also very beautiful, with amazingly clear skin and luscious lips. The realization that Fate had designed this woman for me and my brother made me look closer at her, as though she were a piece of art.

I looked at her the way I'd never looked at another woman, allowing myself to see the lovely curve of her cheek, her elegant neck and, of course, the incredibly voluptuous body that was meant to be adored from head to toe.

Laura doctored up the small white dog until Cotton was relaxed and gently snoring on the table.

"Thanks for that," I said as I moved forward and scooped up the small dog and the dreaded cone of shame.

Laura shuffled forward and lifted her head slowly. "So, what were you saying about going somewhere today?"

I grinned, unable to stop the flood of pleasure her interest created.

"My parents are having a massive late afternoon barbeque. Really, we eat from three until midnight so giving it a title is hard."

Laura's eyebrows rose high, her mouth turning down. "And why would I go to a family function with you, Tyler?"

The fact that she remembered my name so easily made me grin again, and she looked away.

"It's probably the best way I have of explaining the sizzle-hand thing. Did you experience it with my brother as well?"

Laura's head snapped around, her mouth dropping open. "Ah... how..." She took a step back as though she were feeling overwhelmed.

I headed for the door to give her some space. The pieces were falling into place. I could feel them as an amazing calm settled over my body.

There wasn't much to question about my fated mate anymore, not for me, anyway. Laura was it. I knew it with every fiber of my being.

However, my stubborn brother might be a different story. "I know it must seem weird, but I promise it'll all be explained this afternoon."

Laura frowned and seemed to get taller as her back straightened up even more.

Ah, crap. What did I say?

She lifted her chin and stared down her nose at me. "I'm not sure I'm comfortable meeting your parents, or anyone else in your family, for that matter. I don't know anything about you, and for goodness' sake... your brother had my sister half in his bed last night!"

Her respiration had increased and her eyes were darting around.

It was obvious she was upset, and considering what had happened with Brandon and Belle, I didn't blame her.

How best to defuse the situation?

"How is Belle this morning?"

Laura rolled her eyes. "Hung over as all get-out, but I managed to get her up, showered, and to university orientation today."

"Oh, that's great. Which college?"

Laura glared at me. "Why?"

I chuckled. "You don't need to worry about me, Laura. Belle is not my type. Not at all... I was just trying to show an interest in your family. You seem close."

She relaxed a little and the temperature in the room seemed to defrost a bit. "Oh, well, we are. Our parents died a while ago, and Belle is a bit... lost. I want to make sure she gets all the opportunities my parents wanted for her. And that includes university."

I smiled at her. "That's really wonderful. I loved college. Some of the most fun years of my life."

Laura nodded and I heard a knock on the door from the other side.

Laura glanced toward it. "I have to go. That's my signal. I'm running late."

Shit!

"Okay... Well, look. Assuming you don't have to pick up Belle, or do anything else for lunch..."

Laura shook her head. "No, she'll be there all day, then she's going home with a friend to go out tonight."

"Great. Then, please join us. Brandon and I have lunch at Sienna's Café on Saturdays. Do you want to join us for an hour, then you can decide whether you want to come meet the rest of Cotton's family?"

I held up the dog and gave her a bright smile.

Laura cocked her head to the side and studied me. I held my breath and met her gaze. If this didn't work, then I'd be back on Monday.

I didn't want to give up on this woman so easily.

She seemed to make a decision as she flicked her wrist around and stared at the wristwatch there.

"Okay, what time?"

I swallowed the lump that rose in my throat, and held Cotton closer to my chest. "What time do you finish? We're usually there around twelve o'clock."

Laura picked up a clipboard, a weird, professional persona settling over her features. "I'll see you guys there at twelve."

She began to smile, then it disappeared as quickly as it had arrived.

She nodded briskly and left the room through the back door.

I paid and left the office.

Once outside, I inhaled deeply through my nose and caught the scent of the sweet summer wind and blooming flowers.

The seasons had changed and my life had finally turned onto the path that I'd been waiting for.

BRANDON

I groaned and tapped the café table with my fingers, the sound both satisfying and annoying. "Why are we meeting her *here*? You know we won't be able to touch her in public the way we need to."

I couldn't think of anything worse than sitting around a table, sober, with a stranger. A woman who was supposed to be our fated mate.

My brother glared at me and in response, I crossed my arms over my chest. I wanted to throw my hands up in the air and walk out. What was Tyler playing at? Seriously? If Laura was *"the one"*, why weren't we taking her home straightaway to find out for sure?

Tyler let out a warning growl as the door to the café opened with an annoying tinkle of the wind chime the owners had hanging over the doorframe.

Laura walked in and my heart leaped against my ribs.

Fuck, that's intense.

I huffed out a breath, trying to release the squeeze on my chest. Tyler, on the other hand, seemed perfectly fine as he stood up and motioned to our potential mate to join us.

I rubbed at the painful spot on my chest. *That better not happen every time I see her.*

It was freaking embarrassing. I could barely breathe.

Laura walked over to us and sat down in the chair opposite me, a pleasant smile on her pretty face.

A pleasurable feeling rippled through my chest. She was even better looking than I remembered.

"Hi again." She nodded at me in greeting, her green eyes showing a strong confidence I didn't usually see in a woman.

I nodded back. "Hey."

What else was there to say?

Tyler sat forward in his chair. "How was the rest of your shift?"

Laura picked up her menu and flicked her eyes over the list. "Pretty relaxed, thanks. Saturdays are a short day for us. What's good here?"

She glanced up and my heart did another massive thump against my chest and my belly rolled with the feeling.

Damn... Calm down.

I reached for my glass of water and chugged some down, trying to chill out. This reaction I was having was just plain strange.

Tyler answered, "Anything, really. Their bison burgers are fantastic."

I turned toward Tyler and frowned at the sound of my brother's high-pitched tone. What the hell was wrong with his voice?

Probably the same thing that's wrong with my heart.

The waitress came to our table and I cleared my throat loudly, lounging back against the leather seat.

"What can I get you guys?"

Laura murmured and pointed to something on the menu. The woman smiled and nodded at her then she took our orders.

"Yeah, just the burger for me."

Tyler nodded and ordered the same.

Wonder what she asked for?

Then, out of nowhere, Laura fixed me with a dark look.

"What?"

Her eyebrows lifted from their downward arch and her mouth pulled into an even grimmer line. "Aren't you going to ask about Belle? Or did you call her already to check on how she was?"

I coughed, slightly embarrassed that I hadn't thought to do so as yet. "No, I haven't. How was she this morning?"

Pain spread through my foot as Tyler stomped down on my boot. I tried not to grimace and pulled my leg hard, Tyler's foot and the subsequent pain disappearing.

"She's hungover... but at the university orientation I've been pushing her toward all year."

I hummed and shrugged, debating whether or not I should wink at the waitress as she set our food on the table. I decided against it. I couldn't figure out what was up with me, but I had to try and rein in this contrary feeling before it overtook everything and ruined things.

Something in Laura's sentence penetrated. "You've been pushing Belle? Why? Isn't that your parents' job?"

I squirted some ketchup on my fries and crunched down on one, waiting for her response.

Laura shrugged and picked up her fork, skewering the salad she'd ordered, and eating some greenery. "Our parents died a few years ago, so I've gotten her through school. She has a stubborn streak a mile wide and I'm hoping more education will help."

I reached for my water again and swallowed the weird feeling that had risen. I shouldn't care what sort of sister she was, but my mother's lessons about family had been drummed into me since the cradle and Laura's maternal instincts were clearly strong.

BRANDON

5

"That was really good of you, Laura," Tyler said and I nodded my head, unable to remain impassive to such a thing.

Tyler was right. Raising her sister after her parents had died must have taken guts and heart—something missing in most of the women I'd known.

She sat forward and shook her head as she changed the subject. "So, tell me about this family... dinner... thing. Do you get together like that often?"

Her eyes flicked between Tyler and me, and I noticed how much longer her gaze lingered on Tyler, rather than me.

Understandable really, considering last night I'd been ten minutes away from having my way with her sister. But still... The negative comparison to Tyler sat like a lead weight in my gut.

She'd never be able to guess what this lunch was about. What we both wanted from her. No human would.

Tyler answered her. "Yeah, Mom and Dad put on a family barbeque at least once a month. They like entertaining, and now they're mostly retired. Since we both moved out, I think they get lonely for company."

I grunted and ate my lunch, a burger with onion rings on the side. Our parents lonely? I doubted that.

"You disagree with your brother?"

I raised my head to find Laura staring at me, her green eyes far too keen and observant.

I swallowed down a bite of food and wiped at my mouth with a napkin. "Yeah, I do. They've always liked having people around. Our whole childhood was filled with friends and cousins dropping by. Nothing's changed. They just have more money and time now."

Laura stared at me for a moment, then looked back at Tyler with a smile.

"It sounds like you guys had a fun upbringing. Much more social than mine. Do you have any other brothers or sisters?"

I grimaced. "Yeah, unfortunately."

Tyler laughed. "Her name is Renee and you'll meet her today if you decide to come."

Enormous pain in the ass that she is.

My phone buzzed with a text. I picked it up and read the message from my father. I looked at Tyler. "Dad wants us to come over and help set up."

Our dad didn't request so much as *command.*

Tyler frowned and looked at Laura apologetically. "Ah, should I send Brandon alone and stay with you?"

Laura shook her head and pushed her salad away. "No, I completely understand."

The waitress left the bill on the table and I pulled out my wallet, flinging a couple of bills beside my plate.

Laura frowned. "No. I'll pay for my—"

"No." I stood up, staring down into Laura's beautiful heart-shaped face. "What, you wanna pay for a tiny salad? Next time, order some real food and we can fight about it then."

She glanced away and picked up her things, standing slowly and facing me with that grim tightness around her mouth again.

God, she's stubborn... why do I love that?

"I'm trying to lose weight," she said, and I could see the hurt in her eyes. I wasn't having that. It was bullshit.

I said the first thing that came into my head. "Why the fuck would you do that? You're perfect just as you are."

The gasp of the patrons around me was loud but I didn't let them distract me from focusing on Laura and driving home the point.

Somewhere inside my head I marveled at the words. I'd always been drawn to skinny little blondes, but somehow, what I'd said was the truth.

Laura was a major turn-on exactly as she was.

Her eyes widened and her pretty mouth opened and shut like a fish.

I took advantage of her silence. "So, you gonna come to Mom and Dad's thing? Make sure you bring an appetite with you; their pig on the spit is top shelf."

Laura stepped away and turned to look at Tyler. "You said you'd explain about the hand thing."

I glared at my brother. "Did he now?"

And how was he going to explain a perfect mate's bond to a human?

Tyler smiled at Laura with genuine warmth and my lion growled and paced inside me. I stepped away, toward the door, uncomfortable with the sensations flooding through me. I didn't like how much Tyler and Laura had bonded already. Being ignored was not a sensation I was used to.

I heard them walk up behind me so I opened the door and inhaled deeply through my nose, enjoying the fresh scent in the air that late spring always seemed to bring.

Tyler was speaking behind me. "It would be so much easier if you came this afternoon. There will be quite a few people there and you'll be safe, I promise."

I rolled my eyes before turning to watch my brother "wooing" our mate. She looked at me for a moment with hesitation, then went back to talking to my brother.

"Why do I feel so safe with you guys? I know I must sound like an idiot, but I feel like I... completely trust you already, and I shouldn't. I barely know you and I'm generally suspicious of people."

The same reason I want to take you home and mate you right now, even though I know it'll be the end of my life as I know it.

Damn fated curse!

Tyler chuckled. "It's all linked to the same thing. Please come?"

Laura frowned, then nodded, crossing her arms over her big boobs in a move that had me swallowing a groan. My cock was stiffening in my jeans faster than a teenager with his first dirty magazine.

Fuck, I wanted her.

"So, you'll come?" Tyler's voice had risen an octave and I rolled my eyes again. He obviously felt the same.

If I didn't know better, I'd think we were both sixteen again and courting our first woman. I'd never felt so uncool.

Laura nodded and sighed, letting her arms drop. "Yes. I think I have to, or this will haunt me. Not knowing."

"Great. Our folks' place is only about five minutes from our house —201 Grange Road, Jasper."

Laura pulled out her phone, typed on it quickly then tucked it back into her bag.

"What time?" she asked, her voice stronger and deeper than before.

"About three?"

Yeah, that's perfect. There'd be a few people there already and she wouldn't feel as isolated.

"Great. See you both then." Laura backed away and slowly got into her car.

I couldn't help mirroring Tyler as we moved forward, shadowing her, making sure she was safe as she waved and pulled away from the café.

As soon as she was out of sight, Tyler slapped me on the back, his feet actually leaving the ground as he jumped into the air.

"We've almost got her!"

I grunted at my too-enthusiastic brother.

Don't count your chickens, dude.

"Women are a lot more complicated than that, Ty. Especially one like Laura. You think we'd get sent a simple mate?" I shook my head. "Let's go."

Tyler gave me a strange look. "You're joking, right?"

I grunted and we headed off to our cars.

I knew why Tyler hadn't believed my assessment. I sounded like a hypocrite. I'd always claimed that women were simple-minded and easy to manipulate.

Well, that may have been the case for the ones I'd met over the years, but it didn't take a genius to know that Laura was special.

If she really was our mate, which I'd find out today, then she would be harder to handle than any woman either of us had ever met.

Laura

I parked my car about fifty yards down from the address Tyler had given me. I couldn't get any closer. There were cars everywhere.

How big was this family shindig anyway?

I stepped out of the car, tugging on the long summer dress I'd chosen to wear.

Why was I even here?

My decision to come made no rational sense whatsoever. I knew nothing about these men, and there was no reason at all to trust them.

Yet, here I was.

The pecan pie I'd made in a nervous flurry when I'd gotten home was still warm. I picked it up from the front seat and locked the car.

Ready? Okay. Just breathe.

I began walking, thinking about the reasons I was here. The main one being I had to know what this ridiculous attraction was all about. How could I have such a subconscious and strong physical reaction to *two* men, and brothers at that? Especially when they were just so different.

I walked along the grassy footpath, inhaling the smell of the mountains around me. I'd thought Tyler and Brandon's house was beautiful when I'd seen it last night, but this place took the cake.

I stood in front of a double-story massive home, with a wrap-around verandah and acres of land stretching out behind the house. My stomach tightened on a wave on anxious nerves. "Wow."

"It's pretty amazing, isn't it?" A chirpy female voice spoke behind me.

I turned around and smiled hesitantly at the tall, gorgeous redhead who had walked up. *Wow*, applied to her, too. This woman was exactly what I had always wanted to be. Gorgeous. Thin. Confident.

"Hi, I'm Renee." The redhead greeted me with a familiar smile, gesturing for me to follow her up the path to the house.

She was obviously family. She was too relaxed and comfortable here.

"I'm Laura."

Renee smiled with genuine warmth and opened the front door as though she owned the place. "What brings you here, Laura?"

My mind whirled as I stepped into the magnificent house that had the feel of warmth and family love about it, even from the entranceway.

"Ah, Tyler and Brandon invited me."

"Oh, really?" Renee asked, her voice rising.

I looked closer at her. Renee didn't have any of Tyler's coloring, but there was something about the shape of her eyes, and her smile. "You're their sister."

Renee chuckled, amusement sparkling in her green eyes. "Got it in one. I'm impressed."

Renee linked one arm through mine and took the pie with the

other hand, holding it up like a waitress bearing a plate. "Let's go meet my parents."

Panic rose.

Shit, no! Where the hell was Tyler?

"Oh, I'm not anyone special... I just..."

Renee laughed as she continued to lead me through the house. "Don't be silly. You have to meet the hosts of the barbeque."

The sound of Renee's voice was as soothing to me as Tyler's presence. Strange.

"Renee, who do you have there?" The melodic voice of a woman who simply had to be the twins' mother rounded the corner and smiled up at me.

But although she sounded like Tyler, Brandon obviously took after her in a physical sense. She had beautiful blue eyes and blonde hair that was the same shade as her son's.

"Mom, this is Laura. Laura, this is my mother, Rosalie."

"Lovely to meet you," I greeted my hostess, stepping a little closer to Renee for support.

Rosalie surveyed me quickly, smiling broadly as she took the pie Renee offered her. "Oh, thank you, Laura, you really didn't need to bring anything."

"Oh, it's nothing. Thank you for having me."

Rosalie bustled off with a smile, then Renee grabbed my arm and dragged me through the house.

"Come on! I'll give you a tour."

We made our way through the kitchen full of laughing women, and into a backyard filled with talking men.

I froze at the intimidating sight. *Whoa, what a family.* There wasn't a man under six feet in the whole group.

"Laura!" Tyler's voice rang out as he bounced up the stairs and onto the deck.

God, he looks good in casual jeans and a t-shirt.

My heart raced in my chest, deafening me as blood pumped in my ears.

"Tyler..."

Brandon crept up behind him, looking like a reluctant school kid being dragged to the principal's office. And yet, when his eyes rose to meet mine, the heat in their blue depths was enough to make my knees quiver.

Not so reluctant after all?

"Brandon..." I couldn't keep his name from sliding off my lips, too.

Renee let go of my arm and I glanced over to see ecstatic smiles stretching across both Rosalie and her daughter's faces.

"I knew you were special the moment I saw you," Renee said, then turned to grin at her brothers.

I stepped toward the men and away from the women a little, the effect calming my nerves instantly.

Tyler and Brandon moved into the empty places on either side of me, the sensation of protection oddly soothing.

"Sorry we didn't greet you at the door. But it looks like you found our family anyway." Tyler took my hand in his and that odd sensation pulsed in my fingers, but this time it was more of a tingle.

I looked up at him, not sure why I felt so safe when surrounded by these men. I let him link our fingers together, his smooth skin testament to working a job that wasn't manual.

"You want a tour of the property?"

I looked from Tyler's face to Brandon's, completely confused about why these two gorgeous men were so happy to see me. But I would hold my tongue for the moment.

While in Wonderland, I may as well see where the rabbit hole led. "Sure. I should also check on Cotton while I'm here."

Tyler chuckled and Renee asked, "Did I miss something?"

Tyler grinned at his sister, but it was Brandon who answered. "She's a vet." Brandon's voice was even sexier than Tyler's, if that was possible. Like liquid chocolate, smooth and deep.

Rosalie's mouth dropped open and Renee began to giggle and put her hand over her mouth.

I looked up at Brandon, his mouth pulled tight. He obviously didn't find it funny. "Is there something wrong?"

He grunted, "No. Let's go."

Brandon led the way, trudging down the stairs and moving through the crowd with practiced ease. "Come on."

Now that was a talent! I could walk behind him forever and never run into anyone.

Tyler escorted me through the crowd, interested glances being thrown our way, yet no one stopped us as Brandon opened the door to the barn.

"You wanna see the horses?"

I grinned at the hulk of a man and stepped into the barn. "Absolutely. One of God's truly majestic creatures."

I stepped away from Tyler and walked up to the first stall, running a professional eye over the stunning dapple gray. The family had good taste in horses and obviously took good care of them. This gelding's coat was sparkling with health. "These animals are incredible. Do your parents look after them, or do you have barn help?"

I leaned against the stall door, my heart kicking out when I saw Brandon staring at me. He had the most intense blue eyes I'd ever seen—so stormy and deep. There was something special about him, and I hadn't worked it out yet.

He coughed. "We all help, but Mom does most of it."

He stuffed his hands in his pockets and scuffed his boot in the dirt floor. He looked like a gorgeous little boy, all nervous and adorable.

I looked across at Tyler to see if his body language was similar, but found him sitting on a hay bale. He was waiting for something.

"Are you going to tell me about the hand thing?"

I glanced back at Brandon, who nodded slowly. He leaned against the wall behind him and my knees almost gave out beneath me.

This man was way too sexy for my own good.

"Yeah, it's something special that only people with our type of connection feel."

My breath caught in my throat and I locked my knees so they didn't collapse beneath me. What did that mean?

"So... it's a sort of chemical reaction?" I hoped that was all it was. My scientific brain struggled with the idea of it being anything else.

Brandon straightened up and nodded. "Yes, but it's pretty rare. The hand touching thing is only the first step. There's a lot more to it."

I bit my lip, not sure I wanted to know the answer to my next question, yet I couldn't walk away now. "Like what?"

He took his hands out of his pockets and twirled one of his hands.

"Turn around and I'll show you."

"Pardon me?"

He smiled like the devil himself and I heard Tyler say, "Brandon, don't freak her out."

I couldn't pull my eyes away from Brandon's face. Everything in me wanted to go to him and touch him, feel that connection again. Yet, I was a little frightened to know how deep it went.

"Laura?" Brandon twirled his hand again and I huffed loudly enough to be heard around the barn.

"Fine." I turned away and focused on the horse. What sort of parlor trick was he going to pull out while I wasn't looking?

Warm hands ran up my arms and I jumped, electricity zinging along my skin. Softer than before but more sustained.

I turned my head to find out which of the men's touch had made my skin tingle and was unsurprised to see the more confident of the twins behind me.

"Brandon, what are you doing?" I asked as I spun around to face the blond Viking towering over me.

He gripped my arms and pulled me against him, the strength of his body undeniable as my belly quivered in anticipation of what he might do next.

"Showing you…"

And with that enigmatic statement, he dropped his head and kissed me. His lips were hot and soft against mine, strong, but unhurried in their movements.

Push him away! You don't even know this guy!

But my hands were already moving toward his chest and up into his short hair. I moved them around to cup his skull and moaned as his tongue slipped into my mouth. His sweet, minty taste overwhelmed every sense. My knees weakened and I sagged against his large, strong body.

He pulled back and my eyes sprung open. Brandon was staring down at me with shock written across his face.

Tyler stepped up next to us and somehow managed to take me from Brandon. One minute I was in the Viking's arms, and the next moment I was with a dark angel.

"What's happening?" I asked and I ran my tongue over my suddenly dry lips.

Tyler had the most angelic face. I had to touch him. I traced my fingers along his smooth jaw, a dreamlike calm coming over me.

Never, even in my wildest dreams, had I imagined a man like this would want to kiss me.

"My turn." Tyler swooped in and claimed my lips with incredible passion.

He kissed me deeply, exploring my mouth with his tongue and lips.

It was completely different from the strength and possession I'd felt behind Brandon's kiss, but it was just as amazing.

My head was spinning when Tyler finally pulled away.

"Wow." I staggered away from Tyler's warmth and landed with a thump on a hay bale. I was kiss-drunk. Something I'd never experienced before in my life.

BRANDON

6

Oh, God, she is the one. Her taste, oh fuck... her taste!

Fire was burning under my skin and I couldn't clear my mind of the memory of the sweetness of her mouth. Every inch of my body desperately needed Laura to touch me again.

I'd never craved such a thing before. True closeness, where I didn't know where she ended and I began.

I wanted to strip off every item of clothing I wore and beg her to lay her hands on me.

How pathetic was that?

"What just happened?" Laura swayed from side to side where she sat on a hay bale, looking intoxicated. If someone from the outside was looking in, they would assume we'd fed her a bottle of whiskey.

I shook my head and growled at my brother. I couldn't talk, and I wasn't explaining this to her. I felt wild. I only kept a grip on my lion thanks to years of practice, and even now, it was barely by the tips of my claws.

Tyler faced Laura and said, "It's proof that you're meant to be ours."

I threw up my hands and walked to the far end of the stable, shaking my head and grunting.

Fuck, Tyler! I thought you'd be more subtle than that.

I strutted back to the place where Ty and Laura sat just in time to see her shocked expression turn to one of outrage.

"What?" she screeched, the sound ricocheting around the barn.

I glared at my brother and stepped up to block the exit so she couldn't get away. Now that I'd tasted her, I knew she was the one, and there was no way in hell I was letting her run from this.

In truth, I'd kissed her hoping to feel revulsion; to dislike the way she kissed me. Anything to assure me that I had not found my mate. That I could continue to live the life of a carefree bachelor.

I'd been wrong. So very wrong.

Laura was mine... and now I never wanted to let her go.

"I'm sorry." Tyler looked contrite. "I shouldn't have said it like that."

Tyler really did have to work on his wooing skills if that was the best he could manage.

"Shouldn't have said that? Shouldn't have said *what?* What the hell is going on?"

Laura was really screeching now, and seemed to be hyperventilating as her breath wheezed in and out.

Tyler was doing nothing to calm her, and I really didn't like the noise.

I strode forward and grabbed her arms, silencing her with my mouth. She gasped and went rigid for a moment, then moaned and sank into my embrace, making my body come alive.

Her taste exploded through my senses, the perfect combination of sweetness and lust. I needed her in every way there was.

Her hands slid under my shirt and stroked my skin. My lion leaped inside me, then settled down to purr. She pulled away a little to whisper against my lips. "Why do I want you like this? Both of you."

I couldn't speak, couldn't tell her that this was Fate. That she'd always feel this way, and that I wanted her more than any woman I'd ever known.

I tried to tell her in a way that didn't include words, and moved my hands down to her ass and gave it a good squeeze.

Lust tightened my groin and made my cock throb.

Fuck, why do I like that so much?

"Brandon? Tyler?" Our mother's voice called out. She was close by and looking for us.

Damn.

I reluctantly broke our kiss and stepped away from Laura, which was nearly painful. I hated the loss of warmth when her hands weren't against my skin any longer.

"Here you boys are."

Our mother stood in the doorway to the barn, her lovely, wide smile on full display as she looked between the three of us.

She gestured to our mate. "Laura. Come with me and meet some of the family."

Laura glanced up at me, her green eyes worried.

I nodded to her and she seemed to slump. She better not expect me to protect her from my mom. That was never going to happen.

To be honest, I wasn't even sure it was possible.

Laura moved up next to our mother, her lovely cotton dress clinging to her curves. That ass called out to me and said, *bend me over and fuck me, please.*

I shook my head and growled in impatience. When would we be able to claim her?

Mom took Laura's arm and looked back over her shoulder at us. "Come on, boys. I think Laura needs to meet some of your cousins."

I groaned and shared a mutually aggravated look with my twin. Our courtship of Laura had been completely derailed. For now.

LAURA

Rosalie took my hand and led me into a pack of men, all related somehow to the two that had kissed me. I glanced around at the group of massive males who were staring at me and heat filled my cheeks.

Why were they all looking at me like that?

"Laura, this is Jack and Scott. Another perfect pair like my boys."

Two pairs of intense eyes swung my way and I tried to take a step back on pure instinct. Only Rosalie's arm stopped me.

The men before me were magnificent, the same way a pair of tigers at the zoo were beautiful.

They were older than Tyler and Brandon, probably mid to late forties, but their aura was unmistakable. Virile, strong, protective males.

Hang on, what had Rosalie said?

"Perfect pair? Sorry, what does that mean?"

Rosalie smiled at me and squeezed my arm tightly, as though to prevent me from going anywhere.

"In our family, some of the men are born as a set of fraternal twins, and we call them perfect pairs."

I glanced at Jack and Scott again and began to see the similarities to my guys.

One was blond, though he was graying now, blue-eyed, extremely muscular, and tall. The other had brown hair shot through with white, brown eyes like Tyler, and was shorter but still fit and lithe.

"You mean because of being complete opposites in looks?" I asked and Rosalie nodded.

"Yes, but it's more than that. Their personalities are opposite, yet completely complimentary too. One will be more intelligent, the other physically stronger. One will be more protective, and the other will be more affectionate. Think of it as having everything you could ask for in a man split into two, so that you don't miss out on anything."

I looked over the men again and watched the way their mouths turned down.

Was their disapproval on account of what Rosalie was saying? Because they weren't correcting her.

Tyler and Brandon had moved closer again, and I giggled a little to see the similarities in the two sets of twins.

"Wow, you guys have strong genes."

The men shuffled their feet and looked anywhere but at me.

Hmm, they did say the truth hurt, but why would such a compliment be a bad thing? They were beautiful, all of them.

"Am I missing something?" I asked the group as a whole.

Scott, the bigger twin, looked at me and answered my question.

"Rosalie left off the most important thing about perfect pairs. The damn curse."

Rosalie *tsked* loudly and held tight to my arm. I was going to have bruises tomorrow if the woman kept that up.

"It's not a curse, Scott! Just because you two followed your gonads rather than tradition, does *not* mean it's a curse. She's still out there, but you have to find her."

Both men rolled their eyes and a rather stunning adolescent female ran up and grabbed onto Scott's arm.

"Dad, we need you for a minute."

Scott smiled apologetically and bobbed his head. "Nice to meet you."

Jack saluted and headed off as well, following the girl who was sprinting off toward the side of the house.

"What's wrong?" I asked, confused by the multitude of emotions radiating around me.

The men had seemed possessive, jealous even, and sad. I turned toward my guys for more details.

Brandon and Tyler looked at each other for a moment before Tyler stepped forward. "Perfect pairs only have one mate. A woman they share, who is made only for them."

When he paused for breath, I gasped, pain pressing down on my chest. He couldn't be serious.

Tyler continued. "But Scott and Jack chose not to do that. They both married and had kids with women who make them miserable. And we…" he paused again, looking back at Brandon before continuing, "are not going to make the same mistake."

They thought I was this… one woman? *No!*

"Are you telling me that you expect me to… do what, exactly?"

I shook my head and blinked several times. I couldn't be listening to this, or understanding it correctly. "You two can't *both* want me!"

But nothing else made sense. Not the feelings… not the kiss…

My voice had risen in both tone and pitch, and for the first time in my life, I felt hysterical. They had to be kidding.

"Of course, we do." Tyler's tone was smooth and placating, so I began to laugh. Then I snorted and giggled. *Very elegant.*

I pried myself away from Rosalie's death grip and staggered toward the house. I felt both woozy and numb. I couldn't stand up straight.

Renee came toward me, grabbing my hand and gently maneuvering me so that I ended up sitting with her on a comfortable wicker sofa on the porch.

The woman was awesome.

"Can you believe…" I wheezed, grabbing Renee's hand, once again feeling intoxicated. Maybe there was something in the air out here.

"What?" Renee asked, sounding excited and interested.

"Your brothers say they both want me. This has to be some sort of cruel joke… It's not possible."

What was it? *Make fun of the fat sister* week?

The thought sobered me pretty quickly.

Renee smiled gently, like one would when explaining something to a child. "Why would it be a joke? You're beautiful and kind, and if that magnificent aura you give off is anything to go by, you'll be a great mate."

Oh my God! They're all crazy!

I pushed myself away from the strange redhead and stood up. My legs were shaky, but I didn't need a lot of strength to make it to the car.

I was leaving.

"Last night Brandon took my sister home to fuck!" I practically yelled at Renee. "Do you know what my sister looks like? She's a blonde version of you! As if men like Brandon and Tyler would ever want someone like me. This is just... ridiculous!"

I could feel Tyler and Brandon nearby but couldn't bring myself to focus on them. "She's a size four, and wouldn't know one end of a horse from the other! Isn't that what men like? Dumb and easy to get into bed? Because I can tell you—that's not me!"

A muffled laugh sounded behind me and I finally faced the two men who had both kissed me mere minutes ago.

I was blinded anger and disgust, mostly at myself, but I leveled my gaze at them instead. "You two will *never* convince me that you want me—not me as I am. Big, loud, opinionated, and I'm certainly not going to fall meekly into some...some..." I struggled to find the word as polygamy didn't usually work this way. "Weird *ménage* relationship!"

Both men opened their mouths to speak and I ran away.

I managed to get through the house, but the front path seemed much longer the second time around, and my heart was thumping as I hurried along the road to my car.

One of them would follow me, I was sure of it. I had to hurry.

"Laura, wait!"

Brandon. Shit. Tyler would have been easier.

I fumbled with my keys and opened the car door just as Brandon caught up with me.

"Don't you dare touch me!" I shouted, and put a hand up in the air like a stop sign.

He halted in his tracks, backed up, and came around my car, talking over the roof to me. "I'm sorry we laid all that on you at once. We didn't mean to scare you off."

Hot tears pricked my eyes to see the big, macho jerk looking sorry.

"What do you mean?" I demanded, blinking rapidly to dispel the hot tears swimming in my eyes. This wasn't fair.

"Look, I didn't believe the legends either, but..."

"But, what?" I looked at him, watching the fidgety restlessness in his hands as they moved from his hips to the car and back again.

"You're special."

I rolled my eyes and huffed. I'd heard those lines before, and not once had they been anything more than empty words. "I don't believe that. Not after last night. You'll never convince me that you could be attracted to me after I know you tried to hook up with someone like my sister."

Brandon clenched his jaw and his blue eyes pinned me with that intense stare of his. "Your sister is a good time. Not the kind of woman you take home to your mother, and I bet that you've never dated a man like me either, so does that mean you can't find me attractive? Would want to take me to your bed?"

I glared at him for a moment, angry at him for summing up my sister so easily. Our parents were dead, and I saw Belle as a reflection of me now.

The problem was though, despite the anger, Brandon was right about Belle. And about me. I'd always been the marrying kind. I just hadn't found a man who wanted to take me to the altar.

I finally glanced away from him and shrugged. He had a point, but I was not going to admit it. "I don't know enough about you to judge."

When I risked a glance back at him, Brandon had tilted his head and was smiling at me. His cheekiness and confidence were obvious in every line on his face. "I'm a builder by trade. I love my family, but they say I've an abrasive personality. I know I can be arrogant and I'm so honest, I've been told I'm cruel. I find it *really* hard to lie. I weigh about a hundred and twenty kilos and the last time I checked,

I only have about four percent body fat. Sound like any guy you've dated before? Am I your... *type?*"

My breath hitched in my throat as my eyes fell to Brandon's massive biceps, and the way his shirt clung to his thick chest. I'd slipped my hands onto his belly while we'd kissed, and I'd felt nothing but rock-hard abs and hot, smooth skin.

I had to be honest. "No, you're not like any of the men I've dated."

"So, should I conclude that I'm not your type? And that you'd never go for a guy like me?"

I looked down at my hands and shook my head. I wasn't going to lie about that, and he made a good point. Maybe it was possible to like something you'd never tried before?

I twisted my keys in my hand and shuffled my feet. I really wanted to go home. I could feel the walls around my composure crashing down and if I wasn't careful, I'd start crying soon.

Brandon spoke softly this time. "I know you need to go, Laura, but I can hear how fast and hard your heart is beating."

What? How could he know that?

Brandon continued. "I know you feel this too—this connection we share. So, please... think about it. We'll be home all day tomorrow if you would like to come by for a beer or something?"

I nodded without meaning to. I already knew where he lived. I lifted my head and said, "I'll think about it."

He gave me another beautiful smile that was so radiant it made my knees tremble. I fell into my car and turned the key in the igni-tion. *What the hell am I doing?*

I waved to the big Viking as I drove off, my heartbeat still thud-ding like the traitor it was in my ears.

7

I LIFTED THE GLASS PITCHER WITH TREMBLING HANDS AND POURED WATER into three glasses before I returned it to the table. I was slightly disappointed with how nervous I was as I looked out the window for the twenty-seventh time.

It was past noon now, close to one-thirty.

Shit!

How long did we have to wait?

"Do you think she'll come?" I called out to my brother again.

Brandon groaned and stalked over to me. "Yes." He clipped me on the back of my head, hard, and pain spread through my skull.

"Ow!" I turned and snarled at him. Brandon was way too calm for a time like this. "Don't you care at all?"

A sound outside caught my attention and I jumped to my feet, my heart thumping against my rib cage. This was it.

"You need to calm the fuck down." Brandon glared at me and headed toward the front door.

A knock sounded and I jumped.

Oh, shit! She's here.

"Hey." Brandon's casual drawl made me roll my eyes. My brother was going to screw this up. I just knew it.

I'd have to balance out Brandon's idiotic behavior even more than normal.

"Hey, back," Laura responded, her husky voice almost flirty in its response.

Hmmm... Okay, Brandon. Good job. I underestimated you again.

Footsteps sounded along the parquet floor, and I suppressed the shiver that ran down my spine when Laura stepped into the kitchen. Her green eyes sparkled with good health, though she was dressed *not* to impress, which was strange. Was she hiding her beautiful body for some reason?

She wore a loose, plain white t-shirt, and long khaki cargos. Her skin glowed, yet there was no makeup on her face, eyes, or lips.

"Hi." She smiled at me and placed a bottle of red wine on the counter in front of me. "Thanks for the invitation."

I grinned back at her and nodded my head, not quite sure how to speak at the moment. Action was probably better. I walked across to the overhead kitchen cabinets and pulled out two crystal wine glasses.

"You want one, Brandon?" I knew the answer, but I didn't want to appear rude by not offering a drink to my beer-drinking brother.

"Me?" Brandon barked out a laugh and headed over to the fridge, pulled out a beer and popped the top with fluid, practiced ease.

I shook my head, but at the same time as I cringed at my brother's behavior, I loved the fact that Brandon was the most authentic person I knew. He wouldn't alter himself to fit in or impress, for anyone.

I opened the bottle of wine and poured two glasses.

"Thanks for coming over." I handed Laura her drink and indicated where we should sit.

She looked delicious, but seemed to be playing down her sensual body as much as possible. It was funny, really, that she thought by wearing loose, plain clothing, I wouldn't desire her. She underestimated my imagination... and my memory.

"I'm not really sure why I'm here," Laura muttered as she sat down on one of the armchairs opposite me.

I sat on the couch and Brandon prowled forward and fell into the armchair closest to Laura.

I responded to her rhetorical statement. "Because you want to know why you feel the way you do."

Her eyes connected directly with mine, and the green seemed to swirl in their depths. "And how exactly do I feel, Tyler?" She placed her wine down on the coffee table and crossed her arms over her impressive chest.

Ah... crap.

I swallowed and thought quickly. How to handle this exactly? I'd done nothing but think about this moment since Brandon told me what had been said yesterday, but now that I was faced with Laura's pouting lips, I didn't want to talk. I wanted to dive over the table and kiss her senseless.

I swallowed down the need and focused on seducing her, wooing her.

"Your heart races when we're around. You're attracted to both of us, despite how different we look, and you feel safe in our presence."

Laura's mouth dropped open and her arms fell so that her hands ended up in her lap.

Yep. Honesty is the way to go.

I waited, my eyes glued to Laura's gorgeous lips as she finally closed her mouth. Then she wet them.

The sight of her pink tongue snaking out to run along her full bottom lip made my blood flow directly to my cock.

"How..." She cleared her throat and her gaze darted to Brandon, before coming back to me. "How do you know that?"

I grinned, thanking my mother for all the stories she'd told us over the years. "It's described in the legends... but it's also how *we* feel. Both Brandon and I are attracted to you to an almost painful level, and when you're touching us, we get a sense of both peace and fire. Like coming home, but being passionately swept up in a storm at the same time."

Yeah, that said it all.

Laura stared at me, then glanced at Brandon. "Is that true?"

Brandon looked away, then rose to his feet and headed to the kitchen for another beer.

Fucking coward.

My twin was way out of touch with his feelings. I opened my mouth to fill the silence, but when Laura slumped like a deflated balloon, I forgot what I was going to say.

Laura shook her head. "I'm still not sure why I actually came, Tyler. I mean... it's crazy."

I smiled at the beautiful woman in front of me, more of her delicate nature showing with each minute I spent with her. She had so much strength of mind, and a beauty that was obviously soul-deep.

I shivered, tingles of sensation skittering along my spine as I drank her in. Laura would love us with passion and intensity. Enough to keep us both happy for the rest of our days.

We just had to convince her of how amazing it would be.

And by the looks of his behavior, the same went for my ridiculously stupid twin, too. He was just being stubborn about admitting it.

"It doesn't matter why you came, just that you're *here*." My voice rose on the last word, my nerves getting the better of me once again.

Butterflies kept emerging to fly around my stomach, making my breath hitch and my voice squeak. I sounded like I was fourteen. It was fucking embarrassing.

Laura stared at me, then shifted in her chair, appearing uncomfortable.

It was obvious that we needed to talk, to get to know one another better. "How long have you been a veterinarian, Laura?"

Her eyebrows rose and I waited for her to answer while watching Brandon out of the corner of my eye.

My twin sat down and began chugging on his second beer.

The biggest day of our life, and he's getting drunk. Fucking asshole.

"Um... about three years fully qualified. I did two years of pre-vet at university and then four more years of specialized vet college."

I did some quick math in my head.

"So, you're... twenty-seven?"

She nodded, interlinking her fingers in her lap and twirling them around like an adorable teenager who couldn't sit still. "Yes."

I grinned and looked over at Brandon, who was also smiling. Hopefully that meant Laura was ready for a family, because God knew, I wanted kids as soon as possible.

It was all falling into place.

"That's perfect, really. Brandon and I just turned thirty-two."

Laura nodded again and continued to twirl her fingers in her lap, looking lost and uncomfortable.

I had to take control of this, but I didn't want to push too hard. "You look really nervous, Laura. Can I help you feel better somehow?"

She shook her head. "I don't think so."

I shuffled back in my chair, trying not to look intimidating.

"Have you got any questions? I can't imagine how weird this must be for you."

Laura looked between us and bit her lip. "I'm trying to get my head around all this. I know it's negative thinking, but I'm already mentally listing all the reasons this can't work."

That's a good sign, actually.

I gestured for her to continue and ignored the grunt my brother gave in response. Brandon must be really struggling with his lion if he couldn't even manage a sentence.

"Well, for one... there are *two* of you!"

I smiled as kindly as possible. "Yeah, and we both want you more than any woman we've ever met."

She grimaced, but plowed on. "But I work so much. What if I can't give you enough attention or affection, or something?"

Wow, that was what she was worried about?

I shrugged. "We'll sort that out. Three-part families like ours have been working for the perfect pairs in our line for centuries."

Laura's eyes lit up a little. "Can you tell me more about the whole perfect pair thing? About you two, and your family?"

I looked over at Brandon and raised my eyebrows.

Your hormones under control?

"You wanna take this one?"

Brandon chugged on his beer, then set it down on the table, empty. "Our family is huge, as you saw the other day. We're all big, loud, and so tightly knit together that Tyler and I have gotten into more fights than I can count, defending our cousins or each other."

Great, idiot. Do you want her to think we're meatheads?

I was surprised as hell when Laura laughed and her eyes lit up. "Renee, too?"

Brandon laughed.

I sat back, feeling the air around us begin to warm up. Like the sun coming out on a frosty morning, the drops of ice melting away.

"Renee? Not since junior high. We used to get into fights for her, but then we taught her how to defend herself, and after she floored a guy in high school, she never got picked on again."

Laura laughed again, the sound like a smooth whiskey sliding down my throat. "I wish I'd had brothers like you at college. I could have used some help."

I smiled. "Needed a guy or two taken care of?"

"Oh, yeah." Laura nodded, then frowned, her face showing signs of remembering something horrible.

I rushed to smooth things over. "Sorry. Didn't mean to bring up something upsetting."

"Oh, no, it's fine." Laura slid back and crossed her arms over her chest like she was blocking us out again.

Fuck!

"What is it?" Brandon's voice was hard and his face looked angry.

Laura looked up and seemed to relax as she stared at me. "It's nothing."

"Spit it out," Brandon demanded and Laura sighed, relaxing her arms but continuing to fidget with her clothes.

"I... I've never been able to keep boyfriends because they wanted me to be skinnier, or whatever. Especially at college. It was," she shuddered, "horrible. They always expected me to change. And I can't. I know you've said I look fine now, but I don't want to lose you as well because you wished I look like Belle."

Never!

I had to say something. "Laura, you're our mate. Fate created you to be perfect for us. I wouldn't change a thing about your size, your shape, or your style of beauty. You're gorgeous."

I stared at my brother, willing Brandon not to say the wrong thing.

Brandon nodded. "You're perfect, Laura, and I can't wait to get my hands on those gorgeous big tits and ass of yours."

Laura inhaled sharply for a moment and my heart sank. Then she burst into a giggle, her cheeks flushing. "Why do I actually believe you? Despite the fact that I have had so much experience with the opposite. You guys have probably always dated tiny women, but you sound like you're telling me the truth. You've never looked at me with anything other than desire."

I laughed and even Brandon chuckled. "Observant, aren't you?"

She shrugged and smiled.

"Well, it's all true and if you ever get worried, you need to remember that you are our perfect match."

Laura relaxed enough to reach forward and take a sip of wine. "Can you tell me about that?"

This was better for me to explain, probably. "A perfect pair, by definition, is a fraternal twin set of men who complement each other. Who have opposite strengths and weaknesses. This is so that we can give our mate everything she needs."

Laura crossed her legs and my belly tightened in arousal.

"Well, wouldn't she be a lucky woman?" Her eyes sparkled as I watched her absorb the information we were giving her.

I continued. "It's us who would be lucky. My perfect mate is beautiful, intelligent, sweet and sassy, with a huge heart. Everything I've ever wanted."

Brandon cleared his throat. "And if she was made for me, she'd be sensual, funny, affectionate, and hot as hell in the bedroom."

I watched Brandon rake his gaze over Laura and she reached for her wine again. "I'm not all that." She took a sip and her cheeks grew rosier by the second.

Brandon grunted. "Bullshit." He stood up so abruptly the chair skidded back on the wooden floor, making a horrible screeching noise. Laura stared up at him like he'd gone mad.

"You wanna see the house? Tyler designed it. I built it."

I gazed at my twin for a moment, dumbstruck.

Brother, you are brilliant!

I jumped up and held my hand out to Laura. "That's a great idea. Shall we give you a tour?"

Laura looked between us, then slipped her hand into mine, the warmth of her skin making me shiver in longing and need. Laura moved to pull her hand away and I flipped our hands around and linked our fingers together.

I didn't want to let her go. "It's okay. It'll get easier. I promise."

Or so I hoped. The tingles still pulsed through me with intensity.

We walked toward the front of the house and I started the tour.

"I designed the front door based on the mountain lions found in the Canadian Rockies."

I made sweeping gestures toward the hand-carved wooden door that still gave me pleasure when I came home.

It was an intricate design that had taken me months to draw, and just as long to find a carver good enough to get it right. On first glance it looked like there was only one lion, but if you cared to look closer, there were three.

"Hallway, obviously," Brandon said, waving his hand around. "A waste of space in my opinion..."

I opened my mouth to rebuke my brother, but he added, "But

Tyler loves them, and I must admit it does give the living room a bigger impact."

Wow, my brother was admitting I was right. That was a first.

We continued through to the huge, open living space with its high ceiling and neutral colors. It was a great room.

"You've seen the kitchen, dining room, lounge…"

Brandon indicated the area we'd vacated and turned left, heading down to where the bedrooms were.

I kept hold of Laura's hand, squeezing tightly as we moved down another brightly lit hallway. I'd taken great pains to use the natural light as much as possible throughout the whole house. Brandon indicated to our bedrooms.

"My bedroom, and Tyler's," he said, pointing. "The main bathroom."

Laura pulled her hand out of my grip, which hit my gut like a sickening punch, but I followed her, afraid to let her out of my sight.

She stuck her head in the bathroom, admiring the large tiles and Italian-made fixtures. "Wow, awesome bath."

"Thanks." I nodded and watched her creep to the end of the hallway.

"What's this room?" Laura pushed open the door to the main bedroom, sunlight shining down the hall and illuminating our angel in light.

I sighed, watching her brown hair show auburn highlights, a halo of light surrounding her.

"That's our bedroom."

8

I wasn't sure I'd heard Tyler correctly, but as I stared at the huge bedroom, his words made more sense. This was the bedroom they'd created for their woman... and them. Their *family bedroom.*

The four-poster, king-sized bed was magnificent, with the same carved lion in the wooden headboard that decorated the front door.

The room smelled dusty and as I moved around the room, Tyler snuck in behind me and opened the sheer curtains, sliding open the massive windows to let in some fresh air.

"Oh, my." I moved toward the windows as though drawn by an invisible force. The light in this bedroom was so bright, and the view through the window was breath-taking.

I'd never seen the Rockies from such an intimate, perfect place.

Tyler chuckled. "Yeah, I know. I designed the house around this room. I wanted to be able to wake up to the view of the mountains every morning."

I nodded, my eyes devouring every peak and beautiful tree. "Then why don't you sleep in here?"

Both men were silent for so long that I had to tear my eyes away from the window to look at them for an answer.

Brandon turned away, shuffling his feet, and Tyler stared at me, his cheeks slashed with red. "Ah, because we aren't mated yet. This room is for when we have our woman."

"Oh..." *My God! Fuck, they're for real.*

"So, you really expect to have just one woman between you both."

Brandon grunted in answer and Tyler glared at him. "It's worked for our kind for centuries, Brandon."

I cocked my head and stared at Tyler in confusion. "Your... kind?" *What did that mean?*

Brandon's head snapped up, his blue eyes glaring at his brother.

Tyler cleared his throat and looked at his feet. "Yeah, well, we'll get to that later. All you need to know is that we want you, and we'd like to show you how much."

Oh, God, I want that, too.

I stumbled blindly toward Tyler, unable to deny how much I wanted them both.

Doing this, going to bed with them, went against everything I believed or knew to be true. "None of this makes any sense, Tyler."

I moved right to him and let a sigh escape as he reached out and pulled me against him. Heat sizzled between us, but deeper this time —more a feeling of recognition rather than the fireworks that had been evident the first time we'd touched.

"I know." Tyler dropped his head and kissed me.

My eyes slid closed as Tyler's soft lips drank from my mouth, his tongue tasting me, igniting my passion.

A second set of hands crept around my waist and pulled me back so that my ass bumped against Brandon's groin.

I broke away from Tyler's lips and moaned, heat spreading through my belly.

"Come here." Brandon turned me and swung me up into his arms as though I weighed nothing.

"No!" I shrieked, grabbing onto his shoulders and kicking my legs. "I'm too heavy."

Brandon chuckled, carrying me easily over to the bed and placing me down on the mattress. "Yeah, right."

Brandon stepped back and kicked off his shoes, then stripped off his t-shirt.

"Holy smoke." I stared up from the mattress at Brandon. He had the body of a professional football player.

His shoulders were wide, his pecs large and square.

God, he was beautiful. And his arms... I shivered at the size of those biceps. He'd be able to break me in half if he wanted.

"What?" Brandon asked, lifting his chin as though in defiance of any criticism I would give him.

I waited, but he didn't continue so I smiled at him. "You have to know how beautiful you are, Brandon. You obviously put a lot of effort into your body."

I gestured to his massive bulk and he ran a hand across his chest, flexing his shoulders so that he looked even bigger. "I like to work out. It makes me feel good."

I cocked my head and watched the way he moved, almost as though he were embarrassed by his size.

Impossible. He can't be worried about what I think about his looks.

I slipped off the mattress and stood, my toes loving the soft, plush carpet beneath. I pressed my hands to his huge pecs, my own muscles shivering with that intense longing that took over every time I touched these men. "You're spectacular, Brandon."

He finally met my gaze, his blue eyes burning with a need I instinctively knew was only for me. "As long as you think so," he said, though he didn't reach for me.

A strange type of feminine power filled me as a tremor ran through Brandon when I ran my hands over his chest.

His skin was smooth and hot, his flat nipples begging for my attention. I reached for the tiny nubs and ran my fingertips over them until they pebbled. Brandon grabbed my white top and yanked it up.

I didn't want to fight him; quite the opposite. So I lifted my arms, letting him undress me with jerky motions.

I didn't care that this went against everything I believed in. The rules I'd lived by. Never sleeping with a man I wasn't in a committed relationship with, let alone all the rules I had regarding monogamy and fidelity.

But those rules were out the window. I'd never wanted any man like I wanted these two. When would I ever get to experience something like this again?

"Tyler, can you pull the curtains please?" I hated how bright it was in this room. They'd be able to see *everything*.

Every dimple… every stretch mark, every flabby, not-right part of me.

Tyler didn't question me. Instead, the light dimmed as though a switch had been thrown. I released a sigh as Brandon reached behind me, unhooked my bra, and dropped it to the floor. My naturally huge boobs bounced out and I held my breath, waiting for Brandon's assessment.

"Damn, you're beautiful."

Heat seared my cheeks. I couldn't have been more embarrassed, or pleased, by his words.

But rather than focusing on my own feelings, I looked at Brandon. And when I did that, I couldn't deny the need I saw in his eyes as his gaze scanned over my huge breasts. I'd never liked my boobs, but what woman was ever satisfied with her body?

"Pants off," Brandon demanded, reaching for my waist band. I brushed off his hands, undoing the button myself and pushing the khakis over my huge hips. They weren't easy to get off.

I wiggled and eventually got them off, slipping my feet out of my flat shoes more easily than the clothing.

I stood up again, still wearing my panties, not sure I wanted them gone yet. I was already so exposed, being the only one naked in the room.

I was standing in front of two of the most gorgeous men I'd ever seen in real life, and they were still dressed.

"Hop up on the bed, Laura," Tyler said.

I walked toward him, completely aware that my thighs would

wobble with each step and behind me, Brandon would see the dimples in my huge ass.

I lifted my arms to cover my breasts and tried to tiptoe so that my fat wouldn't jiggle too much.

A growl sounded behind me and I stopped halfway between the men, glancing back to Brandon. "What's wrong?" I asked, lifting my boobs up a little more.

"Wrong?" Brandon adjusted himself in his jeans, but didn't make a move to remove them. "You're fucking hot, Laura. Hurry up, would ya?"

I choked out a laugh and shook my head. Brandon was crazy. He must be.

I turned back to Tyler, hesitantly letting go of my tits, and reaching out for him. "How are you so beautiful too?" I asked, wanting him to know I enjoyed looking at his magnificent body as much as Brandon's.

He was smaller in stature than Brandon, but still cut and muscular. He looked fit, as though he could run forever and lift a car when he got there.

I ran my palms up his arms and cupped his shoulders, the muscles bulging out beneath my fingertips.

Tyler smiled at me with what felt like all the warmth of the sun. "I'm not beautiful, Laura, but I love that you want to give us both compliments. Thank you."

He led me to the bed and Brandon hurried over, pushing me back so that I was on the mattress.

I was so nervous I could barely breathe, but my body was ready for this. For them.

This was the stuff fantasies were made of and I was about to experience it for real.

LAURA

9

I giggled with a mixture of nerves and anticipation, and moved into a more central position on the huge bed, laying my head on one of the pillows.

I was really going to do this—go to bed with two men, and brothers at that!

I put out my hands. "Are you two going to join me or just stand there staring?"

The men shared a look before they crawled onto the mattress.

Brandon slid over me and used his knee to spread my legs. "Open for me."

I lifted my legs and wrapped them around Brandon's still denim-clad ass. Heat pooled between my thighs as he took control of the situation. I hated to admit it, but I kind of loved his dominant attitude.

Brandon kissed my lips and I reached up and dragged him down so that his chest was flat against my breasts. Tingles flared between us as his tongue speared into my mouth. I groaned with pleasure as he tasted me.

"I'll squash you," he said against my lips.

I laughed a little. "You're kidding. I love the feel of your weight on me."

I pushed down on his back and encouraged him to lay on me more.

He slowly released some of the weight he was holding on his arms and let his body sink onto me.

A contented bliss settled over me and I sighed. "Yes."

Brandon moaned and dove down to kiss my neck, biting and sucking the flesh along my throat, then moving further down.

I closed my eyes, unable to stop the whimpers that escaped me as his mouth seared a path of heat and pleasure down my body.

I ran my hands through his short hair, touching him as much as possible as he made his way toward my breasts.

His wet lips slid over my flesh as he cupped one of my breasts with both of his massive hands and plumped it up for his mouth. The kneading sensation was comforting and arousing at the same time, and I opened my eyes to watch him enjoying my flesh.

He sucked the nipple into his mouth and I cried out as pleasure shot through my belly to center between my legs. He suckled me over and over, then moved back onto his haunches to stare down at me with a grin.

Some sort of pleading noise left my mouth without permission, and then I reached out for him with both hands.

"Come back, please." I needed his heat and weight on me again.

"No, it's my turn." Tyler muscled his brother out of the way and reached over to pull my knickers down my legs.

I let him, impatient for more. It had been so long since I'd been touched by anything other than my vibrating toys.

"Wow, you're even beautiful here." Tyler ran his soft fingertips over my sensitive clit and down between my folds, making my whole body buck up.

I gasped out a response, "That's impossible, but thanks."

I wasn't waxed or overly concerned about keeping that part of myself manicured. I didn't have time or the inclination to be pretty only for myself. Although, the longer Tyler stared at my pussy the more I thought, maybe I should have made some kind of effort.

Brandon stood so that he was shoulder to shoulder with his brother and both of them stared down at me.

You've got to be kidding me!

Their twin stares excited me, even as embarrassment rose. I tried to close my legs, but Tyler held them wide open with his hands on my thighs.

Brandon shook his head and chuckled.

I didn't like that at all. "Don't laugh at me." I sat up and tried to twist away from them.

Brandon fell forward and pinned me back onto the bed, then he rolled onto his side and cupped my mound with his hand.

I turned my head away, not wanting to look at the smug son-of-a-bitch and Brandon chuckled again, his lips moving to my ear. "I keep waiting for something about you to turn me off, but you have the best-looking cunt I've ever seen."

I hissed and turned around to glare at Brandon, but it didn't stop him talking. "You do. It's a beautiful pink, the lips are symmetrical, and it has the most inviting slit I have *ever* seen." Brandon shifted his hand and pressed two long fingers into my opening.

I cried out as he stroked me deep inside. Wave upon wave of pleasure flowed over me, my eyes closing to better enjoy the sensations.

Brandon didn't stop. He fucked me with his fingers and I sobbed with every stroke. Damn he was so good at that. I grabbed for his arms, swept up in the most intense pleasure of my life.

"Let's see how responsive she is," Brandon said as he curled his fingers and something lit up inside me. He groaned. "Oh, good girl."

I let another moan escape and Brandon kept fucking me with his fingers until the tension inside me tightened and built to breaking point.

Then Tyler joined in, his hands stroking my thighs as Brandon fuck me deep.

"Oh, fuck, Brandon... Tyler... please..." I tossed my head from side to side, digging my fingernails into Brandon's arms. I wasn't sure what I was begging for, but I hoped one of them knew.

Brandon pressed deeper, hitting that special spot once again, and spoke into my ear. "Come for me, my woman."

I screamed as the tension peaked and broke, bringing with it the most intense orgasm of my life. My body shuddered uncontrollably as Tyler's hands stroked my hips and thighs while Brandon pressed kisses to my neck.

"Good girl. Damn, you're so sexy." The words were growled at me, deep and guttural. Almost animal-like.

I took that for the compliment it was.

Brandon was crude and dirty in the best way. He'd push my limits every day in the future, I could see it already.

I turned my face toward him and kissed him, wrapping my arms around his neck, and pulling him as close as I could.

TYLER

I stared down at my woman and my big brother wrapped in a passionate embrace after Laura had orgasmed in Brandon's arms. I'd always assumed my brother would be a good lover. After all, he'd had enough practice, but for the first time in a long time, I was glad to be a perfect pair with him.

A wave of happiness caught me unawares, making my throat tighten and tingle with unshed tears. We'd found her, *finally*.

All that pointless dating. Finished.

All those nights of cold comfort. Gone.

We had reached our destination and the sunshine was warm. My hands continued to stroke Laura's creamy thighs, and I watched as they opened automatically for more.

Oh, yeah. It's my turn, my mate.

My mouth watered as her juicy, wet cunt opened and revealed her pink lips, swollen from her orgasm.

Brandon's hand moved up her body to play with her breasts, and

I slipped onto my stomach so that my face was inches away from her mons.

I inhaled deeply and moaned as her musky scent filled my nostrils.

"Yum." I extended my tongue and swiped it through her folds, my breath rasping unevenly as her deliciousness spread across my taste buds.

I'd never tasted anything, or *anyone*, like it. *Wow*. I dropped my head and began to eat her out properly, with the appetite of a starving man, because I was. Laura was the richest wine on the planet, and I'd been surviving on dirty water.

She cried out and reached down to dig her nails into my head. "Fingers too. Please, Tyler."

I grinned against her beautiful pussy lips and brought my hand closer to her opening. She needed penetrating, *got it*, and *fuck*, what I wouldn't give to be able to sink balls-deep into her right now.

But Brandon and I had already talked it over and decided the best way to earn her trust and affection was to be selfless this first time.

Laura was the most important woman in the world to us, and she needed to know that beyond a shadow of a doubt.

I traced the pink, swollen opening with my fingertips and focused on suckling her clit as I slid two thick digits into her channel.

"Fucking hell! Oh, crap!"

I looked up to see Brandon holding down a thrashing Laura, her body heaving with shudders.

He held Laura's wrists to the bed above her head and dropped down to kiss her. She moaned and surged up to meet him.

I looked down at the swollen, juicy cunt in front of me. This was it. The last pussy I'd ever see, feel, taste.

And it was the most beautiful thing I'd ever experienced.

I moved my fingers in and out, reaching inside her, and pressing on the textured little bit of flesh partway up her vagina. A muffled groan sounded and I teased it over and over while I flicked her clit with my tongue.

A high-pitched cry flew into the air above me as Laura tensed her entire body, her legs straightening on the bed on either side of me.

I licked faster, feeling her pussy tense around my fingers, then with another hoarse cry Laura began to shake. Her cunt squeezed in waves of spasms and a light cream coated my tongue as she came.

Oh, fuck, that tastes good.

I licked her clean as she shook with the aftermath of her latest orgasm, and I slowly withdrew my fingers.

I could hear Brandon whispering to her, so with a final kiss to her spectacular pussy, I crept up the bed and took the almost-comatose Laura into my arms.

"I... you... what?" Laura's eyelids fluttered like she could barely keep them open. Her eyes were glazed over in a bliss that made her look drugged. I could only hope that she became addicted to Brandon and me, because now we'd never let her go.

"Sleep, sweetheart, we're here."

She settled her head against my chest and almost instantly her breathing changed into the even patterns of someone who had fallen into a deep sleep.

"I'm about to burst over here!" Brandon said with a growly groan.

I grinned at the frustration in his voice. I knew exactly how he felt.

I let my own eyes close. My cock throbbed against the fly of my jeans, but I was content.

In an emotional sense, anyway. I couldn't feel better.

"Well, go fix yourself somewhere else. I'm staying here."

Brandon made some gruff noises but he soon settled on the bed behind Laura and lay an arm around her.

Despite my buzzing body, we all must have drifted off, because the next thing I knew, I was waking up to Laura shifting uneasily in bed.

I kissed her head. "You okay, honey?"

She pulled back a little to blink up at me. "I need to pee."

I chuckled and forced my lethargic body to roll off the bed, pointing in the direction of the ensuite bathroom. "In there."

I watched Laura quickly gather up her clothes as she shuffled to the bathroom, looking far too self-conscious for a woman who had broken apart in our arms not so long ago.

"Where's she going?" Brandon's groggy voice sounded from the bed.

I looked at my sleepy twin. "Bathroom."

"Hmm." Brandon let his head drop back against the pillow and I stretched, feeling oddly settled and peaceful.

Laura stepped back into the room, looking shy and a little haunted. "I'm sorry I fell asleep like that. You must think I'm very selfish. Can I... you know, help you both now?"

She lifted her eyes finally to mine and I could see the guilt there.

Wow.

She actually cared about our feelings. Felt guilty that we'd pleasured her and not had satisfaction ourselves. Since when did our lovers care about anything other than their own pleasure?

I knew Brandon was a bit more selfish than me in bed, but I'd lost count of the times my lovers had left me aching.

I gave her the biggest smile I had in my repertoire. "Are you kidding me? Watching you come apart was incredible. You don't have to worry about anything, you've already given us so much pleasure tonight."

A charming blush rose in her cheeks and a lovely smile graced her beautiful face. "So, what happens now?"

Brandon slid onto the end of the bed. "Now we date. Tyler and I want you, and we wanted to show you today how much. We're not fooling around here. We want you to give us a real chance."

Fantastic. Well said, brother!

"We've got your number, so we can message and call. Maybe catch up for dinner or something?" I suggested, and watched Laura light up like a Christmas tree.

"Really? I mean, this wasn't a one-time thing?"

Brandon and I laughed, the sound so natural and loud in the room that had lain vacant for so long.

I walked forward and cupped Laura's face, kissing her soft lips as gently as I could. "Would you like to stay for the night?"

Laura looked up at me, her green eyes wide and open. There was no façade, no hiding of the feelings she was fighting.

Her heart and soul were there for me to see, and it was a wonder that such a person would be so vulnerable. "What time is it?" she asked, turning to see the clock. "Oh, shit! We slept for two hours."

I looked at the clock and took a step back. That was incredible.

"I'd, um, like to go home if that's okay? My sister will need help with her university paperwork, and I need to think about a few things, too."

I took her hand and walked with her to the front door, wanting her to feel happy to come and go as she pleased.

Brandon followed us down the hallway.

"No problem. You do what you have to do. We just wanted to make you feel good."

"Oh, you did! It was amazing." Laura stopped walking and stared at me, then looked over to Brandon behind me. "It really was. Thank you so much. Both of you."

Brandon stepped closer and Laura let go of my hand to turn toward my twin. He pulled her into his body and kissed her like a drowning man clutching at air.

I tried not to laugh out loud. Brandon could say what he liked, but there was proof in the pudding right there.

Over drinks, over the years, Brandon had often boasted about what sort of women he liked in his bed. Those women who'd open their mouths, or their legs for his cock, and preferably didn't want to kiss or cuddle after.

Yeah, right.

So much for the twin who didn't enjoy kissing and avoided connecting with his lovers.

We were both already so in love it wasn't funny.

Laura and Brandon finally pulled apart, their eyes soft and their lips red.

"You sure you don't want to stay?" I asked again, watching Laura share a heated and almost desperate look with Brandon before tearing her gaze away.

"No! I have to go, but thank you for the best afternoon of my life."

I swallowed the lump in my throat as we walked Laura out the door and to her car. She climbed in and gave us a bright, huge smile before waving and heading off to her responsibilities.

My chest ached as I watched her drive away.

"Well, that went better than expected," I said as we walked in the front door once again.

Brandon hummed noncommittally and headed off to his own bedroom. An uneasy feeling spread through my gut as I remembered that, up until a few days ago, Brandon hadn't been ready to settle down with a mate.

Oh, I'm begging you brother... please don't ruin it for both of us.

And with that disturbing thought, I walked into my office and sat down to try and concentrate on some work.

LAURA

10

"Hey, Belle! Are you home?" I called out as I walked through our family home, the one for which I'd taken over the mortgage when our parents had died.

"Yeah. Yeah, I'm here." Belle's tone wasn't good, which put a dampener on my high.

I walked into the kitchen area to find Belle sitting at the dining room table with a huge catalog in front of her.

"Hey," I said, sitting down at a chair opposite her.

It was Sunday night, and I really should be getting an early night for work tomorrow, but I could already see this was going to be a late one.

"How can I help?"

Belle just groaned and threw up her hands.

Nine years my junior, Belle had been a miracle baby after several miscarriages. My parents had doted on her, and she was a bit of a spoiled princess in every way.

I hadn't helped, since I'd pretty much written her college application and helped her with every project or assessment she'd ever done.

"I just don't know what to do! What to choose! This is too hard, Laura."

Her classic catch-cry.

"We'll sort it out, don't worry Belle-Belle."

I pulled over a class schedule and roster and looked at the choices she had available for next year. Basic English, math and general science courses would be appropriate for a Liberal Arts major.

"Where have you been?" Belle asked, and I looked up to see her peering at me like a specimen under a microscope.

"What do you mean?" I tried to smile casually, but knew I was failing as Belle looked at me with a disapproving frown.

"I mean... you have a post-sex smell and look about you. What gives? Spill. I didn't know you were seeing anyone."

I struggled to hide my shock, and then the smile that rose on my lips afterwards.

"I didn't have sex." *Technically.*

Belle gave me a *yeah, right* look. Her mouth twisted up and she opened her eyes big and wide.

"Okay..." I rolled my eyes so that I could glance away. "So I may have done something this afternoon, but it's new, so I don't want to say anything."

Belle slapped me across the upper arm. "Tell me! This is so exciting! You haven't dated anyone in like... forever! Spill."

What did I say to my sister? She'd gone home with Brandon, probably to have sex with him. How did I tell Belle that he now wanted to date me?

"Well... I... the guys... um..."

Oh my God, and I considered myself articulate.

"Guys? As in more than one of them?"

Belle looked shocked, but so interested, I laughed. "Yeah, there's two of them."

"You're seeing two guys at the same time? Whoa, Laura! Since when are you a hussy?"

Heat flooded my face. "It's not like that. I... well..."

How did I explain it?

Belle gave me her entire focus, and all my worries came flooding over. "Okay, it's time for me to ask for your help Belle-Belle."

"My help? Since when?"

I laughed. "Since two brothers decided they both want to date me."

"Oh, my."

I clapped my hands on my cheeks to cover the blush I could feel spreading across my face. Just saying it aloud made me want to keel over with shame.

"Yeah. I know. It's ridiculous."

Belle, my airhead sister, cocked her head at me. "What do you mean?"

"I mean..." How much did I reveal to my sister?

I weighed the pros and cons and realized that this was the moment I needed to decide whether I was diving headlong into this pond of ridiculousness, or if I was backing away slowly.

"I mean... I mean, who would want me, Belle? I'm over the hill. I'm twenty-seven. I'm fat. And two *hot* brothers have declared they both want me."

"Do they want you to choose between them?"

This was the harder part to admit.

"Ah... no, they want to share me."

Belle's mouth literally dropped open.

My stomach twisted and tightened with nerves as I thought about what I had to say next. "And that's not the bad part, Belle."

"What's the bad part?"

I took a deep breath and plowed forward. I'd always been one to rip a band aid off. Fast.

"One of the guys is Brandon... the guy you went home with Friday night."

I expected retribution, curse words and horrible things said. But instead, Belle blinked at me and said, "Who?"

I stared at her. Did she literally mean, who was I talking about? Or was she being funny?

"Brandon. You know, the guy I had to rescue you from on Friday night? When you were super drunk and..."

I trailed off. Had I been worried for nothing? Did Belle even remember him?

Belle flicked her long hair over her shoulder and stuck her nose in the air. "I don't remember much about Friday night. I know I went home with someone, so I have to assume he was all right to look at, but I wouldn't be able to pick him out in a line-up."

"Oh my God." I let my head hang down as I laughed to myself. "I was so worried..."

When I looked up again, I had to wipe the tears from my eyes, amazed to find how much better I felt off-loading my guilt over Belle.

I hadn't realized how worried I'd been about this part of the equation.

"I thought you'd be upset with me."

"Upset? Because you want to date a guy I kissed when I was drunk, or—I didn't do more than that, did I?" she asked.

"I don't think so," I replied.

I could always ask Brandon for clarification, but from what I gathered, he'd taken her home and she'd started vomiting.

Nothing else.

Belle reached out and grabbed my hand. "Are you sure about this, Laura? I mean, it's not like you to date two guys at once."

I burst out laughing. "I know! It's not like me, at all! I don't know what I'm thinking, but I..."

"But you, what?"

For the first time in forever I saw a hint of maturity in my baby sister. My mother's stoic strength.

"I want to give it a try. Even if it's crazy, even if every part of me says that two guys like that should not want a woman like me."

"Like you? You mean beautiful, fierce, super-intelligent and successful?"

Whoa. That's how Belle saw me?

"No, I mean, I'm... fat."

Belle groaned and rolled her eyes. "Not all guys like skinny,

Laura. And you're way prettier than me. I don't know why you've been single for so long, but if you've finally found a guy, or guys, who like you for who you are, you should go for it. Or them."

For the first time in two days, true hope flared in my chest.

"When did you get so smart?"

Belle shrugged and indicated back to the university schedule notes on the table. "I'm not. I can't even decide which courses I want to take."

I smiled and pulled forward the large university catalog. "Let me take a look."

For the rest of the evening we talked about Belle, what she wanted to do with her future, and which dorm she would move into in the fall.

But meanwhile, my head was spinning. The main hurdle for me being with Brandon and Tyler was looking to be more of a log to leap over.

I glanced down at paperwork in front of me, something else niggling at the front of my mind. "Hey, Belle."

"Yeah?"

"Do you think I'm a slut?"

Belle guffawed. "You? Are you serious? How long has it been since you even kissed a guy?"

Before today? "I don't know, a few years probably."

"Exactly! So how can you even ask me that?"

I glanced down and away from the baby sister I'd raised. I didn't want her to think less of me. Ever.

"I mean... If I do decide to date them—Tyler and Brandon—will you think I'm a slut?"

Belle grinned. "Laura, you know me. I say, do what makes you happy. If two brothers wanna spoil you and love you, why on earth would you say no?"

I looked at my sister and stared at her, bewildered. "But don't you think I'm weird? Strange? Immoral?"

Belle shook her head and shrugged. "Whatever you want, Laura, is fine by me. I mean, as long as you're all consenting adults, who the fuck cares anyway? It's not like Mom or Dad are here to comment."

That thought brought a lump to my throat and an ache to my heart. No, they weren't, but they'd probably have something to say about it.

"They'd hate it, wouldn't they?"

Belle grinned. "I don't know. I accidentally stumbled across a suitcase of theirs one day. I was looking for a duffle bag, and instead found all sorts of stuff! Dildos, blindfolds, butt plugs. The whole shebang."

"Oh my God... you're kidding me?"

I'd never thought of my parents as being kinky, in any way.

"Nope, wish I was. But look—long story short, I don't think you can guess what Mom or Dad would say. As far as I know, they only wanted us to be happy... and safe."

I reached over and squeezed her hand. "You're right. So, let's see about getting you settled for school."

Belle rolled her eyes and we spent the next two hours talking about university and which dorm she'd move into. After several years of being my sister's guardian, I was finally going to get my life back.

FOR THREE DAYS, I FLOATED AROUND THE CLINIC WITH MY MOOD ON CLOUD nine. Brandon sent me dirty, crude, super-hot messages every day, while I got the most beautiful, heartfelt texts from Tyler.

Every time my phone beeped, I'd play a game with myself and guess who it was. I could never decide who I wanted a message from more.

I quickly realized that I wouldn't be able to choose between them, even if I had to. It was just like Tyler and Brandon's mother had said last Sunday. Between them, they had every base covered. I couldn't imagine ever needing something that these two men couldn't give me.

"Hey, Laura. There's a Tyler in the waiting room asking for you."

I couldn't help the smile that spread across my face when the receptionist told me I had a visitor.

He's here.

"Thanks."

What did he want? I walked through the clinic doors and into the waiting room with eyes only for the beautiful man standing in the center of the bright, white room. "Hey, Tyler."

He grinned that mega-watt smile he possessed and walked toward me. Every part of me ached to reach out and touch him. My fingers actually tingled with longing, yet my need to be professional in front of my staff and patients won out.

"I was hoping you'd have time to go out for lunch?"

"Oh, well…" I did have a longer than normal lunch break today. "That would actually work. I had a few last-minute cancellations."

LAURA

11

Tyler stepped forward and I pressed my lips together to stop the giggle that rose as I took a few steps back, away from him.

There were people sitting in the waiting room and their interested eyes followed me, including the gaze of my receptionist. I had three patients remaining to see.

"Give me half an hour, and we can leave." I grinned at him, unable to keep the excitement out of my voice. Despite all the messages lately, Brandon, Tyler and I hadn't been able to pin down a date to catch up again.

I'd had work and Belle to sort out, and they'd had work, gym and family stuff too.

My next three patients were easy cases, thank goodness, since my brain was a bit preoccupied.

Each time I entered a new room or got a glimpse of the waiting area, my belly heated up and a sudden awareness prickled along the back of my neck.

Thirty-five minutes later, I stuck my head into the now-empty waiting room, grinned at him and held up a finger. "Just give me one more minute."

Then I twirled and practically ran to the staff room.

My vet tech, Mary, was there getting ready for her lunch break. "Who's the hottie, Doc?"

I took off my white lab jacket and grabbed my handbag. "Tyler.

He's an architect."

I turned and headed toward the door, amazed at the words that had just left my mouth. I sounded like a snob, only interested in money and prestige, which I wasn't.

So I added, "And the biggest sweetheart on the planet."

Mary grinned at me. "Slept with him yet?"

I waggled my fingers at the cheeky younger woman. "Bye, Mary."

I pushed through the door, hearing the giggle behind me. I stepped into the waiting room and walked over to Tyler. "Ready?"

Tyler slipped his hand into mine and nodded. "Yeah. Let's go."

The sensation of his skin on mine sent a shiver of longing through my body, but that initial electric current was blessedly gone.

Tyler looked at me with interest. "How's your day been?"

I forced myself to relax a little. I'd never been pursued by any man like this before. His enthusiasm made me more excited than it probably should have. My natural instincts said to trust him, and compounded by all the things I'd learned from his mother, I wanted to allow him into my life.

"Really good. No problems so far. How 'bout you?"

Tyler's eyebrows rose up a little. "Ah, good, thanks."

I squeezed his hand. "Any interesting projects you want to tell me about?"

We walked into the local café and sat down in a corner booth.

"Hey, Laura. The usual?"

I looked up at the familiar face and beamed. "Yes please, Tania. Tyler, I highly recommend any of their grilled sandwiches or the all-day breakfast."

Tyler scanned the menu, then dropped it back on the table. "The Rockin' Big Breakfast and a chocolate milkshake, please."

Tania smiled and moved away with a wink at me.

Freaking small towns.

This would be the talk of the town and my friends for the next month, which I kind of understood.

I hadn't openly dated anyone since moving back here after my parents had died and I finished vet school several years ago. This was going to be an epic problem if things didn't work out. I hated people asking personal questions, and I could imagine the commiserative words I'd get from everyone if they found out I'd been dumped.

I shook myself and tried to focus on something positive. "So, tell me about your job."

Again, he gave me that weird look—part confusion and mostly surprise. "Okay. Well, I'm currently designing an art gallery in Toronto."

Now that is cool!

"Oh, wow. So, the lighting and height of ceilings is really important?"

Tyler's eyes lit up and he leaned forward. "Yeah, as are the materials we use for constructing the building, since so many artsy types want to be as green as possible."

I sighed as my own big breakfast was served in front of me—no mushrooms and extra bacon. The rich scent of the cooked meat wafted up and I picked up my knife and fork, saliva gathering in my mouth.

No more salads for me. Screw it.

"Wow. That sounds amazing... challenging, too, which is great. Nothing worse than being bored or not enjoying your job."

Tyler chuckled and began eating with gusto, the food disappearing off the plate and down his throat as though he were inhaling it.

I took a few bites of my lunch and had a sip of my fragrant peppermint tea. It was so nice to slow down and relax a bit. Most of my lunch breaks were spent reading notes or answering phone calls. I rarely sat and really became present in the moment. When Tyler didn't continue, I cocked my head and asked the question burning in my brain. "Why do you seem surprised that I want to know about your work?"

Tyler looked up at me, his brown eyes sparkling. "I'm not sure I should say anything."

I shrugged and continued to eat. I wasn't in the mood to push at the moment. My empty belly was filling with warm food and I was settling into the booth so comfortably, I was considering never moving again.

"It's just…"

I glanced up and waited for him to continue.

Tyler cleared his throat. "I've never had a woman care about my work, let alone one be clever enough that I could discuss concepts and ideas with her."

I shrugged again. "So, you've been dating the wrong women."

Tyler burst out laughing, the sound so rich and beautiful it caused shivers of awareness to creep over my skin.

He shook his head and went back to eating with a sigh. "Ain't that the truth?"

I ate as much as I could, which wasn't as much as normal, thanks to the jumping frogs inside my stomach. I laid my cutlery aside and picked up the cup of tea. I nursed it in my palms, warming them on the heated porcelain.

"Tyler, what did your mom mean about you and Brandon being destined for only one mate?"

Mate was such a weird word to use.

Tyler stilled like a deer caught in the headlights, then began to move again, slowly and carefully. "She meant that because we were born a perfect pair twin set, Brandon and I won't be happy unless we find a woman who will complement both of us."

I nodded, cross-referencing all the information I had and still coming up short. "But I've never heard of twins being described as a *perfect pair* before, and polygamy is illegal."

Tyler sucked down his milkshake and placed it back on the table. "Our kind are rare, and the general population wouldn't know much about how we do things."

Were they in some sort of cult or something?

"You mean you all worship some demigod and have six wives?"

Tyler laughed again, loudly enough to draw stares. Heat flooded my cheeks, yet I remained focused on the man in front of me. "No, not at all, but good guess."

My cell phone beeped and I glanced down to see a message from the clinic. A few swipes and presses later and I groaned. "I've gotta get back."

A dog had been brought in with a snake bite. I was needed ASAP.

Tyler stood up and moved over to the counter, paying the bill before I'd even gathered my things and made it to the front of the café.

"Thanks so much for lunch, Tyler; you didn't need to do that."

We made our way out the front door and began the short walk back to the clinic. When the building came into view, Tyler stopped us both. I turned to say goodbye and Tyler lifted his hand, stroking my cheek with his fingers.

I couldn't resist the urge to touch him also, so I reached up and cupped his jaw, drawing his face to mine for a kiss.

A soft, purring noise escaped his lips as I nuzzled his cheek and kissed the spot beneath his ear.

What the hell is that noise? Brandon does that, too!

"What *are* you, Tyler?"

He drew back and stared down at me, his brown eyes wide and searching. I held his intense gaze and didn't back down. There was something different about Tyler and Brandon, and it wasn't just the fact that they believed in weird ménage relationships, like some sort of backward sister-wives.

"I... don't know what you mean." Tyler stepped back and swallowed awkwardly, his throat working hard.

I placed my hands on my hips and tapped my foot against the concrete.

I didn't like being lied to. I was a big girl, I could handle the truth, and I'd prefer to hear it now, before I fell head-over-heels for these guys.

"Yes, you do. You said something about our relationship being normal for your kind? What kind is that, Tyler?"

Tyler took another step back and bit his lip. I continued to stare at him, putting as much strength into my "schoolmarm" gaze as I could.

He'd crack. I'd make sure of it.

"We're..." Tyler cleared his throat with a rough cough and looked around as though checking to make sure no one was listening.

Then he squared his shoulders. "We're animal shape-shifters."

I tapped my foot again. *What a crock of shit.*

"Seriously, Tyler, I trusted you to tell me the truth and you come up with some bullshit like that?"

My rage mounting like a boiling pot, I turned around and marched back to the clinic. I must have been kidding myself to believe I was special to them.

Tyler's strong hands grabbed my arm and whirled me around before I made it to the front door. "I'm not joking, Laura. Would you come to our place for dinner tonight and we'll show you?"

He didn't look like he was lying. His eyes were guileless, his hands moving over his hips and thighs with restless, anxious motions. The longer I looked at him, the more I saw the truth.

He actually looked hurt that I didn't believe him.

Oh my God... maybe he meant it... metaphorically?

I huffed out a breath and tried to be as reasonable as possible, considering the circumstances. "Okay, I'm sorry. But you cannot expect me to believe that you are a... what did you say?"

Tyler let go of my arm slowly, as though expecting me to bolt again. "Animal shape-shifters. All of my family can turn into mountain lions."

Shock had my mouth gaping open before I closed it with a snap. "You've got to be fucking kidding me."

Tyler shook his head. "No. It doesn't change who we are, it's just... an extra skill we have. We have full control over our lions when we shift. We're not dangerous to you at all. Promise."

I stared at him as I struggled to wrap my mind around what he was saying. I blinked and waited for the apparition before me to disappear. "I... ah... don't know what to say, Tyler."

He stepped away, lifting his hands in supplication. "Don't say anything yet, just keep an open mind. We would never hurt you."

I nodded numbly, my mind falling all over itself to assemble the broken jigsaw puzzle in front of me. They'd had me alone more than once, and if they'd wanted to hurt me, they could have. As far as my safety was concerned, I believed I could trust them.

"Um, what time should I come over?" *Seeing is believing, after all.*

His story was crazy, but what proof did I have that he was lying, other than my belief in the normal laws of biology?

But then again, there were many things in this universe that I didn't understand, and I'd been wrong before.

Tyler stepped closer. "Do you want to come for dinner at seven?"

I opened my mouth to agree, to get this lunacy sorted out, then my memory kicked in and flashed up my schedule for the day. "Crap. I'm doing a late shift tonight."

I frowned and tapped my foot again, thinking quickly. "Okay... let me work this out. I brought something to eat from home, so I'll eat before my last surgery and head to your place after. I should be there about eight-thirty."

Then I could sort this shit out, once and for all.

Why do all the good-looking ones have to be crazy?

Tyler's mouth quirked up into a half grin. "You won't regret it, Laura."

Hmmm, not so sure about that.

"Can I kiss you goodbye?" he asked, his tone tentative.

I shrugged and looked away, not sure how I was feeling and whether I wanted him to touch me at the moment.

Tyler's warm hands cupped my jaw and tipped up my head, his touch instantly soothing my nerves. His soft lips touched mine with a reverence that made my resistance melt into a puddle at my feet.

Then he pulled back and kissed my nose in a protective way.

I sighed and reached out for him, holding onto his waist, and resting my head against his shoulder as that strange wave of contentment stole over me.

Tyler stepped away after too short a moment and I looked up, wanting him back as soon as my hands held nothing but empty air. Despite everything that had been said, my heart still yearned for this man.

"See you tonight, beautiful."

Then he turned and walked away.

I couldn't help the way my gaze dropped to his ass. Those buttocks clenched and moved in his jeans in such a way that made him just delicious.

My belly gave an almost vicious clench and I groaned, pushing myself away from the wall and heading toward the front door of the clinic.

It was going to be a long afternoon.

BRANDON

12

I soaped up my hands and massaged my balls, groaning with the ache that throbbed in my gut. I needed a fuck. A good, long screw.

"Then why the hell did you turn Stacey down again, you idiot?" I muttered to myself and rinsed the soap off the rest of my body.

Stacey was hot and she was easy. I just called her over and fucked her whenever I wanted, and best of all, she came all over me when I did it.

It was always satisfying, but also, pretty fucking dirty.

Yeah, and not in the good way.

I growled in disgust at my own inner monologue and stepped out of the shower, toweling myself down and heading into my bedroom.

"What time did Laura say she'd be here?" I called out to my twin, my voice deep and rough.

I'd never felt this unsettled before, even when I was twenty-one and *wild*. I wanted to run. I wanted to fight, and oh, God, did I want to fuck! But, obviously, I didn't want to fuck just anyone, anymore. Now that I'd met Laura, I couldn't get her out of my head.

Adrenaline raced through my blood like wildfire, strong and persistent and insane.

This is all Laura's fault.

"About eight-thirty," Tyler called back.

I looked at the clock. Eight twenty-two. Not much longer and she'd be here. In our home, where she belonged.

I pulled on some new, tight jeans and a white tank top that clung to my chest, foregoing any underwear. That'd only slow her down.

I glanced in the mirror and flexed my biceps to make the muscles bulge. I knew Laura liked my body, and that made me want to show it off to its best advantage. I wanted to make her happy.

I adjusted my stiff cock in my pants and groaned as pleasure tingled over me. "I think she's here."

I closed my eyes and tilted my head to listen. An engine shut off outside, and then a car door opened and closed. Shoes scrunched on our path out front.

The doorbell chimed.

Yes!

I opened my eyes and rolled my shoulders, as though getting ready for a sparring match. *This was pure torture, like nothing I'd ever felt before. I didn't know how to process everything thrumming inside me. If I couldn't release some of this tension soon, I felt like I might burst into a million pieces.*

Tyler had headed to the front door so I padded out into the living room, feeling my cat raise its head and purr. She was here.

Laura stepped into the hallway, walked along the hall and into the sunlit living space. My heart kicked out like a horse's hoof against a barn door.

I groaned with discomfort and pressed a hand to my chest. Why did this woman make me feel like this? Like I was all tied up in knots?

Laura's lovely, long hair was tied up, harshly drawn back away from her face. Her usually glowing skin was pale and slightly sweaty, yet I don't think I had ever seen her look more beautiful.

"Hey, Brandon." Laura cocked her head, as she did when she was thinking. "You okay?" she asked, concern written all over her face as she studied me.

She dropped her bag and started toward me.

My shifter leapt up and took control of my mind.

I hadn't been expecting it so fast, and I gasped as my throat began to close. I pushed down with all my strength, but for the first time in over a decade I lost the battle. My control slipped through my fingers like a dream disappearing into the night.

"Tyler!" I managed to call the warning to my brother, hoping he'd be able to handle what I was about to do to my mate.

I groaned with pain as I staggered back, feeling the shift come upon me.

My shirt began to rip and the jeans I was wearing were going to fall straight to the ground.

Every inch of my skin heated and changed, golden fur sprouting out as I fell to my knees, my human limbs morphing into the strong legs of a mountain lion.

I looked up to see my brother holding our woman. She was staring at me in silence, her mouth gaping open and her eyes wide.

I stared back at her through my lion's eyes, damning myself for slipping like that. Such an adolescent move.

Instantly, I dropped to the floor and lay down like a domestic house cat in the least threatening position I could manage, then I flicked my eyes up at her.

Laura continued to stare at me, but at least she hadn't run shrieking from the house. Something within my shifter self stirred to life. I began to purr with happiness, my lion content to finally be within reach of his mate.

"It's okay, Laura." Tyler's voice was low and meant to soothe. "I'm sorry, I meant to explain *before* Brandon shifted, but he obviously couldn't control it."

Laura stared at me unblinkingly and I stared back. I didn't dare move in case I spooked her. I'd never forgive myself if she ran now.

"He...what?" Laura began to shuffle, moving back and forward on her feet like someone deciding whether she wanted to run or stay.

Please stay, sweetheart. I need to feel your pussy around my cock at least once.

I was feeling calmer now that I was in my lion form. My blood was cooler, and I could feel my humanity within reach. It was time to shift back. We needed to talk.

I sat up and leaned back on my hind legs, let the shift back happen naturally. Watching my brother with Laura in human form made me yearn to touch her, too, with my hands.

I rolled up and into my body, feeling my bulk stretch and fill out my skin. My clothes were in a puddle on the floor and I didn't want to step back into them.

Laura screamed and bolted around the couch, holding onto the leather seat back with both hands as she glared at me. "Don't you ever do that again without warning me first! Do you understand?"

I laughed, shocked into humor by Laura's unusual reaction. She was mad because I hadn't warned her I was about to shift?

Fuck, I loved that woman.

Then my thoughts penetrated my consciousness.

Love?

No! Oh, hell no.

I sobered quickly and nodded. "Yeah, okay." The fact that she was referring to the future made me smile, but I tried to remember how strange it must be for her to see such a thing.

Laura blew out a breath and stood up straighter, her hands finally relaxing their death grip on the couch. "Okay, wow. Okay..."

I looked to my brother for help. What were we supposed to do now?

"So, okay. Your family—all of them? They can all do that?" Laura rattled off the questions, her voice high and squeaky. I watched her with pride. She was obviously confused and freaking out, yet she was *still here.* She got major credit for that.

"Ah, yeah, they can," I said, when Tyler didn't seem inclined to speak.

"Okay, okay..." Laura began to pace, muttering to herself. "So, it really is true. My... whatever you guys are... you turn into mountain lions. I can deal with that. Surely, I can. I am a vet, after all."

A hysterical giggle burst out of her, before she turned to stare at

Tyler and then me with wide, bright eyes. I was beginning to feel uncomfortable standing in the middle of the room, naked. If we weren't going to get into anything, I'd better cover up.

"Oh, wow." Laura's eyes ran up and down my body with greedy intent and my cock reacted. I groaned as heat and blood flowed to my groin and I began to harden.

I released a gasp and reached a hand out to the woman who *supposedly* was my perfect match.

Let's see how you handle this, beautiful.

"You gonna help me out with this, Laura?" My voice was raspy with need. "Because I've been hard for you since the minute I laid eyes on you."

Laura's tongue snuck out and wet her full pink lips, making them glisten. I may have been pushing her a bit too fast, but I needed her and I wasn't afraid to let her know it.

Hell, the way my cock was now standing at attention, it was impossible for anyone in the room *not* to know it.

When she didn't step forward, I reached down and began stroking myself. Hot, hard flesh ran between my fingers as I stared into Laura's green eyes.

She looked hungry and aroused. Why wasn't she moving?

Tyler cleared his throat. "Brandon, you probably need to go fix that yourself. I think Laura might be in shock."

My heart sank. I'd hoped that Fate would send me a woman who was perfect for *me*. A woman who could handle *every* part of me, especially my high sex drive. I let my cock go and my erection immediately began to fade with the rejection.

I turned away from them and started toward the hall, disappointment sitting like a lead weight in my gut.

Laura strode across the room and cut me off before I could reach the door.

"What?" I was afraid to ask more. I didn't want to be rejected twice in the space of a minute.

She reached up to cup my face and narrowed her eyes. "I still have so many questions."

Was that a yes to my earlier request?

I ran my hands down her arms, fighting the need to take her hard and fast. "I'll answer any questions you have later, sweetheart. You just need to give me a kiss first."

Her worried expression cleared and she tilted her face up for a kiss. I met her halfway, tasting the delicious nectar of her mouth and letting go of all restraint. I pulled her into my naked body and let the moan escape as she opened her lips and let me in.

After a minute or two, Laura pushed on my chest and I released my hold so she could pull back.

I let her go. If she wanted to stop there, I'd do as Tyler suggested and go take a nice, cold shower.

"You okay?" I asked, trying to be gentle.

She nodded and reached for my dick, gently stroking the shaft up and down, and watching me with huge eyes. "Should we take this to the bedroom, my big lion?"

No words had ever sounded so sweet.

I heard Tyler's growl of approval.

Laura smiled. "You look a little wild."

More than a little. I huffed out a ragged laugh and took Laura's hand in mine. I couldn't speak in that moment, so I tugged her out of the living room, hearing her giggle as she jogged beside me to keep up with my urgent stride.

"You know my legs are shorter than yours, right?"

I guided her down the hall and into the end bedroom. I'd never take Laura to my old bedroom. I'd had other women there, and that was now in my past. The future was this bedroom, where Laura was *ours,* and she'd always be loved in this room where no ghosts lay.

Not love! You're screwing her, remember?

Fuck...

I shook away the internal thought as we entered the bedroom

and I turned to pull Laura into my arms. No matter what word I placed on it, I was going to be inside her tonight.

"I want to feel your pussy wrapped around my cock."

Laura shivered in the circle of my arms and looked up at me with trusting eyes.

"You want that too, don't you, beautiful girl?" I waited for the affirmation, a part of me needing to hear the words that would solidify what her actions had already shown.

"Yes." The word was whispered, but in the quiet room she may as well have screamed it.

I crushed her mouth with mine, my hands grabbing her luscious ass and dragging her against my naked body.

Tyler's hands slid around her breasts, making her moan, and he began kissing her neck.

Laura pulled back suddenly and dropped to her knees.

I couldn't help staring at her.

That was unexpected.

When she looked up at me, my stomach tightened with an emotion I couldn't identify.

"I want you too much, Brandon. I know this first time should be a bit slower, but I'm aching."

I nodded and gripped her head, drawing her toward me. What a thing to hear from my mate! I didn't care if it was slow or fast, long or short, I just wanted *her*.

"You can have anything you want, gorgeous woman."

Laura moaned as she slid her hot, wet lips around me and sucked hard, drawing me in like quicksand.

"Oh, fuck. Laura." I couldn't drag my eyes away from her face as she swallowed down my cock.

She moved with an enthusiasm I'd never seen, and I couldn't look away from the picture she made. She was addictive and my coming orgasm dragged on my control which was already precarious.

Fingers of pleasure danced along my spine as she moaned and

moved on me. She looked so damned innocent as she gazed up, making eye contact while her mouth was full of my dick.

What a contradiction!

I pulled my cock out of her mouth with a quick jerk, my body so close to coming that I made it by a mere second. I blew out my breath, my body still throbbing with the strain of having to stop the inevitable topple into orgasm.

"Up. Now."

I didn't care if I sounded like a caveman, uttering single-word sentences in a tone lucky to pass for human. I wasn't afraid to admit how primitive I felt.

It obviously didn't phase Laura as she jumped to her feet and looked at me with a cheeky grin on her face.

I kissed her again, unable to stay unconnected for a single moment.

She moaned and opened her lips, meeting my seeking tongue with her own. Her orange-flavored taste exploded through me as I pressed my cock against her belly. I needed to be inside her, feel the very core of the woman who had bewitched me.

I pulled back and tore at her clothes. I'd been dreaming about her lush curves and gorgeous cunt all week. Work had been a fucking nightmare when I'd been fighting an erection all damn day.

"I need you naked, Laura."

Laura stepped back and with a few fast moves, she had her work clothes pooled at her feet. Now, she stood in front of me in red underwear, the lacy bra cups enticing my hands to lift and caress her huge boobs.

"My turn." Tyler stepped around me, now naked, and I stifled the growl that rose. I'd forgotten for a moment that my brother was even there.

I stepped toward the bed and sat down to watch the erotic show happening in front of me.

Tyler unhooked Laura's bra and slowly revealed her curves, licking her skin and suckling on her nipples when they came into view. She panted and moaned, leaning back and holding Tyler's head as he feasted on her.

I couldn't resist reaching for my cock, stroking it slowly as I watched Tyler pleasuring our lover. Not one pulse of envy passed through me. If anything, my arousal continued to simmer, holding strong, yet waiting for my turn to burn.

Tyler knelt on the floor, pulling her lace panties down and delving his hand eagerly between her thighs. He stroked her gently, exploring her flesh. "You're so wet for us already."

His ground-out words punctuated Laura's moans as Tyler moved his thumb over her clit to make her pant and gasp. Her panties hit the floor and I inhaled, the air rich with the scent of Laura's arousal.

Tyler pressed open her thighs and she spread her legs for him. He set his mouth to her pussy and she reached for his head, her knees looking like they were about to buckle.

Better step in.

I stood up and walked around them, pressing into Laura's back for support, wrapping my arms around her indented waist.

She cried out and leaned back against me, gasping her pleasure as Tyler continued to lave her clit with his tongue.

"Oh God... Oh, Tyler."

I slid my hands up and cupped her full breasts, tweaking her nipples as she tipped over the edge and began to shudder, screaming out as her orgasm took her.

She shuddered in my arms and I kissed her shoulder, my own body throbbing in need for this sensual woman Fate had chosen for us.

When she relaxed and settled against me, Tyler kissed her small patch of dark hair and stood up, pressing his lips to hers in a reverent caress.

"Let's get her on the bed." Tyler spoke to me over her shoulder and slid his arms around her, lifting her easily and laying her down on our bed.

She smiled and stretched her arms above her head like a cat who'd eaten the cream.

I grinned down at her. *We aren't done with you yet.*

I walked around the huge bed, crawled across the mattress, and patted the center. "On your belly here, Laura."

She rolled over, looking hot and flushed, yet strangely satisfied as she moved into the position I wanted.

Oh, yum... She looked absolutely delicious laid out before me.

I ran my hand down her spine. Such smooth, soft skin. Such amazingly succulent curves of flesh, all flowing smoothly over her body.

I loved it all.

The curve of her spine, her plump ass, her long legs. All of it spoke of femininity and fertility. My lion wanted to mount her, bite her, claim her, and I realized with a small amount of surprise, so did my human side.

I lay over her back and set my teeth to the side of her neck.

Laura arched up so that her spine was plastered against my chest and panted out, "Harder, please."

Oh, hell yes!

I slid my fingers over her hip and cupped her ass, loving the feel of the flesh in my palm. "Fuck, you're hot," I told her before doing as she asked and sucking her neck harder, knowing I was marking her and loving the feeling of it as her salty skin filled my mouth.

I grunted and bit her harder, exulting in the way her hand came up and cupped my head to hold me closer.

I needed to be inside her.

Now.

BRANDON

13

I SLID ON TOP OF MY MATE AND SPREAD HER LEGS WITH MY KNEES. She tilted her pelvis up and bumped her ass against my stomach in an invitation as old as sin itself. She wanted me too, and both parts of me, both the shifter and the human, wanted to cry out in relief and gratitude.

My heart pumped blood fast along my veins as I moved back and pulled Laura up on her knees so that I could stare at her pussy.

"Oh, fuck, that's beautiful. So hot."

I spread her cheeks and watched her pussy open for me. Her juices glistened against her lips and lit the way to heaven.

"Stop looking at me." Laura tried to move and close her legs.

Paradise was disappearing. "No way. You're fucking beautiful."

I looked over at my brother and tilted my head. Tyler slid onto the bed and kneeled next to Laura, holding out his cock to her.

Not what I was meaning, but good enough.

"Would you suck me too, gorgeous?" Tyler asked.

She looked over her shoulder at me, worry furrowing her brow. I grinned at her. "Suck him, beautiful. Then I get to fuck your luscious body and make you feel good."

I ran my fingers between her legs, tracing the wet contours and pressing on her clit, making her gasp. I loved how responsive she was.

"Protection?" she asked.

I shrugged. I didn't want anything between us.

"We can't carry diseases... because of the lion genes. But I'll pull out for pregnancy protection."

The last thing we wanted was a baby to complicate things.

Something wild flashed in Laura's eyes for a moment. "I'm on the pill for health reasons. If you're sure you're healthy..."

I nodded again. "I promise. I wouldn't lie."

"Okay then." Laura stared at me for one long moment, as though assessing my honesty, then she looked back at Tyler.

The old fears washed over me. I'd never left my seed inside a woman before. Mostly because I didn't trust any of the others not to get pregnant, but also because I reserved that closeness for my mate.

Our mate.

But did we want to assume everything was fine, already?

Probably best to wait and see.

Laura opened her mouth for Tyler and my twin slid his cock straight between her lips. The sight affected me like it was my own cock getting sucked. My flesh ached and hardened, even with no contact.

I glanced away, sounds of pleasure filling the air as I continued to stroke Laura's clit and she made Tyler groan.

I didn't know why I wasn't diving straight in after all this waiting, but then my mouth began to water and I realized I needed more. "I need to taste you."

I fell to my stomach and slid my tongue over her clit. It was swollen and slick, tasting of honeysuckle and sin—a perfect combination to make my head spin. I flicked over the beautiful bud until Laura was crying out to me.

"Brandon! Please!"

That's what I needed to hear.

I kneeled behind her once more and set my cock head to her entrance. I inhaled, savoring this moment. Then I slowly pressed the throbbing shaft into her pussy.

Laura moaned around Tyler's cock and pushed back against me, the move so carnal and hot that I growled deep in my chest.

Control! You're not a fucking horny teenager anymore!

I gripped her hips and held her there, rocking my pelvis so only the head entered her. Over and over again I flexed my hips, torturing myself and Laura with too-shallow penetration.

She was tight and hot, so sweet and too perfect.

Everything I'd feared she would be.

Everything in me silently screamed that I'd found who we'd been looking for.

Too soon, you idiot. Too early to be sure.

"Do you want it, baby? Do you want my cock in your juicy cunt?"

I continued to rock gently, letting her have the first few inches and controlling it with every bit of strength and willpower I had.

The moment had to be unforgettable for both of us. I never wanted her to forget the first time I took her.

"Yes! Brandon! Please!"

Laura pulled her mouth off Tyler's cock long enough to speak, and her pleading tone was everything I could ever want.

I grinned, grabbed her hips and thrust home.

Laura came, her back arching up as she pressed back against me, her pussy clamping down on me so tightly it felt like she was trying to squeeze my cock off.

I panted and gripped her hips hard, reining in my orgasm. As long as I held still, I had hope.

Come on… come on. Don't. Please.

It just felt so damn good!

When I regained enough control to continue without blowing on the spot, I pulled back and slammed in again. She was perfect. So exciting in her moans and the way she tilted her pelvis up for me.

I began to fuck her… really fuck her, and she took it. Each thrust made my balls bang against her ass and pleasure ricocheted through my body, starting at my cock and spreading out in waves of sensation.

Sweat dripped down my back as I thrust deeper and deeper, feeling a flowing connection between us that was hard to put into words.

I couldn't seem to get close enough to her.

I heard a cry and looked up to see Tyler come in Laura's mouth. Our greedy little girl swallowed him down and finally drew back to look over her shoulder at me.

She smiled, then turned away, dropping her head down on the bed and reaching back to connect with me. She linked our fingers together at her hip where I held her and a jolt of electricity shivered along my arm, like the closing link of a circuit falling into place.

Laura fell forward and tilted her hips up, crying out as I gripped her hard and fucked her until she screamed. "I'm going to come again. Oh, *God*!"

Her pussy clenched down on me and I rode through the waves until my own ocean crashed down upon me.

No hope stopping it this time.

I pulled out with only a moment to spare, pressing the head of my cock to the base of her spine and coming over her creamy skin in hot spurts that made my eyes roll back in my head.

"Oh. My. God."

Exhaustion swept over me at a rapid rate. I could barely stay upright. I swayed on my knees where I knelt behind her.

Tyler was already laying down next to Laura, whispering to her, loving her.

I staggered to the bathroom, toweled my sweating face, wet a washcloth for my lover, and made it back to the bed. I wiped Laura's back clean and threw the square of material toward the bathroom.

Made it...

I fell onto the bed and crawled up to her, drawing Laura onto my chest with the last of my strength. Tyler settled in behind her. I took deep breaths to slow my thundering heart and tried not to make conclusions about my future.

~

LAURA

I blinked back tears as ecstasy threatened to consume my heart.

Never had I experienced such intense feelings of belonging, of rightness. I was exactly where I was supposed to be, lying between these two men, and precisely who I was meant to be with. This was the most perfect moment of my life.

I lay with my head on Brandon's shoulder, his arm around my waist and his lips caressing my forehead. I could feel Tyler's calming strength snuggling me from behind. "I don't...I can't believe..." I bit my lip as tears welled again in my eyes.

Pull yourself together.

Brandon chuckled and wrapped both arms more tightly around me, the feeling of love and warmth from both of them swarming my senses until finally, I stopped trying to hold in my emotions. Tears slid down my cheeks unchecked.

Yep, lost the battle there.

"You don't believe what?" Tyler asked as he kissed the nape of my neck and stroked his hands down the tingling skin of my back.

"What is it, baby girl?"

I smiled at the deep sound of Brandon's voice and rolled so that I had my head on his arm and I could look at both of them.

"I can't believe how amazing that was. I mean, it wasn't just good sex, it was earth-shattering."

Tyler smiled and ran a finger down my cheek. "I'll be inside you next time."

Brandon didn't move one single millimeter beneath me and I frowned at his silence. I looked up to see his expression had turned stony, then back at Tyler's soft face. Something uncomfortable swirled within my belly.

"You aren't jealous, are you?" I asked, more to Brandon than Tyler, but I let the question sit between both of them. "I assumed you were comfortable with this because you two suggested it."

Tyler smiled at me. "There's no jealousy, love—none."

She looked up. "Brandon?"

His generous mouth twisted. "No, that's not a problem."

Then what is it?

"Is it what I said that's worrying you? Is it always that amazing for you guys?"

Brandon grunted and began toying with my hair, stroking it over my shoulder and twirling the strands between his fingers.

Thanks, caveman. Eloquent response.

Tyler leaned forward and kissed me, moaning as he tasted my lips with his tongue, then drew back. "That was the most incredible sex of my life, Laura. You are an amazing lover."

Relief filtered through me, his compliments as welcome as sunshine on a stormy day.

I giggled in delight and gasped when Tyler began teasing my breasts with his fingertips.

I turned to Brandon and looked up at my blond-haired god. He wouldn't look at me, concentrating on my hair instead.

I'd work him out, but for the moment, I was giving him the benefit of the doubt.

I grinned at them. "It's not me who's amazing! I've never come like that before. So hard and fast. How did you know how to do all the right things?"

Brandon finally met my gaze, his blue eyes guarded as he shrugged.

Tyler grasped my chin and pulled me to him. He shook his head at me. "It wasn't us. It was you. I can't speak for Brandon because we've never shared a woman before, but no one's ever responded to me like that. Our chemistry is amazing."

I lifted my hand and cupped Tyler's jaw, a part of my attention still concentrating on the silent man at my back. "Thank you, my love."

Tyler's eyes widened, then his face melted before I could call back the words. Damn... I was in *so deep* with these guys.

Now to deal with the moody, silent one.

I rolled onto Brandon's supine body. His hot skin pressed into my breasts, frissons of pleasure dancing along my nerves where we connected.

I placed my hands down on either side of his head so I could look directly into his amazing blue eyes.

"Fuck, you're gorgeous," I blurted out, and watched my man's cheeks flush with heat.

How did this big Neanderthal get so affected by such simple compliments?

"Thank you for giving so much to me, Brandon."

He grunted and reached up to draw me down, kissing me deeply so that continuing my speech was no longer possible.

I'd have to wait for the words from this one.

I knew he wanted me, and I felt loved and safe in his arms. Time would tell if he really was the partner I needed.

Finally, I pulled back to draw breath and a yawn escaped my mouth. "Sorry."

Brandon chuckled and twisted us so that I ended up in front of him, my back to his chest, both of us lying on our sides.

"Sleep," Brandon demanded. "I get up at five and I'm gone by five-thirty. What time do you need to head off, beautiful?"

Heat stole across my cheeks as pleasure lifted my heart. He wanted me to stay.

Tyler lay on his side facing me and took one of my hands with his, linking our fingers and stroking my cheek with his other hand.

"Ah...about seven-thirty."

Brandon's hand stayed tight around my belly, and I began slipping down into sleep until a thought shot into my brain.

I couldn't believe I'd been distracted away from such a momentous revelation. My eyes sprung open. "We didn't talk about the lion thing!"

"Trust me, it's not going anywhere. We can talk about that anytime," Brandon said, shuffling closer, his pelvis tucking into my ass and spooning me from head to foot. Even his shins ran along my calves.

I let out a sigh as tingles spread through my body. I relaxed against him like a piece of pasta under boiling water.

"You're a perfect fit." His tone was joking, yet I heard the words and knew they were true.

I wiggled my ass, settling in properly and let my eyes close.

I supposed I could wait until morning to talk about the animal thing. What was the difference? They weren't going anywhere and neither was I.

"Yeah, you're pretty perfect, too."

BRANDON

I woke up at five like clockwork, with a sense of warmth and happiness filling me. *That's new.*

I blinked in the darkness and became aware of the difference. There was a soft female body pressed against my chest and groin, my hand still possessively cupping her warm, silky thigh.

I usually woke up cleanly and quickly, ready to get up and go as soon as my eyes were open.

This morning, however, I leaned forward and inhaled the smell of Laura's hair and let my eyes slide shut again.

I'd never felt like this before—warm and happy. *Home.*

Within my chest there was a small amount of panic fluttering around the edges of the contentment that dragged at me like a delirium fever.

I eased back from the warmth of the cocoon the three of us had made in the center of the bed with reluctance still tugging at my heart.

This bed was so much more comfortable than my other mattress, and hopefully now that we'd shown Laura who we were, she'd move in with us and we'd sleep here from now on.

Yeah, simple. Right?

I crept across the carpet and glanced back to see Laura wriggle closer to Tyler, obviously seeking to replace the heat I'd provided.

Fucking work.

I swallowed the frustrated groan in my throat so I didn't wake them up and went to my bedroom and bathroom to quickly shower and dress. By the time I stepped out the front door and got into my truck, the sun's light peeked across the mountains.

Something was missing. I checked the essentials. Wallet. Keys. Cell phone. Yep, all present.

Then what could it be?

I searched inside myself, then huffed out a laugh when I realized what it was.

Every day for the past decade, I had been battling something akin to depression. I'd never admitted to it to anyone, and had certainly never spoken the words aloud. Not even to Tyler.

I'd filled the void with alcohol, work, friends, exercise and sex.

But it was always there, eating at me whenever I was alone.

I sat in the driver's seat and searched for the black hole that had been chasing me for a decade like a relentless Pac-Man.

"Fucking hell!" I burst out laughing, the sound coming from deep within my gut as I started the truck.

It was gone!

Who'd have thought that finding my mate would fix *that*?

I drove to work filled with peace and an excitement for my world that I'd never felt before.

TYLER

14

I blinked awake, my cock throbbing against my belly with a morning hard-on.

"Good morning." Laura's smiling face beamed at me as her hand explored my shaft with confident strokes and caresses.

I rolled on top of her, knocking her flat as our bodies connected.

Her legs opened with invitation before she wrapped them around my waist and her elegant fingers slid up my arms and around my neck, keeping me close.

Damn... what a wake up.

I shivered at the intent in her moves and love flowed through our connection. I dropped my head to kiss the soft lips she tilted up for me.

I whispered against her mouth, "I love how you do that."

Laura arched her back to get closer, her huge, soft breasts pressing into my chest. "Do what?" she asked, running her hands through my hair and making my scalp prickle.

I shivered again as hot sensations slid over my skin.

Then Laura moved her hips so that my cock butted up against her opening. I pressed my pelvis forward and found her wet and hot. "Touch me like...that."

I gasped loudly as I slid into her warmth, the hot clasp of her body making me want to blow from one stroke.

Oh, wow. She feels even better than I imagined.

"Ahhh..." Laura dragged her nails along my arms and tilted her pelvis up for a deeper penetration. I panted for breath as waves of pleasure rolled over me.

I held onto my control through sheer will and began to thrust.

I rolled my hips in a way I hoped she'd like, aiming for contact with her clit with each downward stroke

I took a shuddering breath, closed my eyes, and lay my forehead against Laura's. Being with this woman was like slipping into a warm bath after being submerged in ice for years.

Her need to touch me, to give me pleasure and share love with me, was such a foreign concept. My previous lovers were selfish, often cold. They'd loved receiving pleasure, but I soon realized they didn't care about me. As long as they received the orgasms they sought, they were happy.

Laura was different and it made me want to growl with a different sort of frustration. All those years of anger and fear, hurt and disgust. I'd walked through a desert with nothing but a glass of water, and now I was in an oasis of pleasure and love.

"Tyler, oh, Tyler, that feels..."

I moved my hips faster and reached down to grab Laura's ass, tilting her up for a better angle.

"Oh, I'm—Tyler!" Laura cried out and squeezed her legs around my waist, forcing me to stay inside her as she came around me.

I clenched my teeth and fucked her harder, riding the exquisite waves of her orgasm right through to the end.

Laura gasped a few more times, shuddering all over, then relaxed under me like every bone in her body had been removed. She stared up at me with a look of wonder and love that pushed me right over the edge.

I pulled out and exploded, groaning against her neck as I collapsed onto her warm body. My cock sent wave upon wave of pleasure up my body as I spurted all over our bellies. Laura stroked her hands down my back, kissing my face and murmuring loving things in my ear. I never wanted the moment to end.

When I finally lifted my head to look at her beautiful face, sleep tugged at my subconscious, beckoned from its dark abyss. "It's still early, gorgeous, let's sleep."

Laura nodded, her eyelids dropping.

"But first, let's clean up."

We disengaged, and I grabbed Laura's hand and gently lifted her up and out of the bed. Her beautiful eyes were at half-mast as I led her into the bathroom and gently cleaned her body.

I loved the look of pure contentment on her face as she hummed and smiled.

I quickly wiped myself clean and guided her back to our room.

We fell back into bed in a tangle of limbs and soft words before slumber claimed us both.

LAURA

I giggled as I received the third message for the day from Tyler. We'd woken late and jumped out of bed in a hurry. I'd showered quickly and dressed in the spare work clothes I had in my car.

Luckily I'd popped home before going to their house the night before and packed a bag... *just in case.* And thank goodness I had or I would have arrived at work a lot later than the ten minutes late I was.

Come over for dinner again. We miss you.

I checked the clock and typed a response while a stupid smile spread across my face. I couldn't remember a time when I'd been this happy.

I'll be there in an hour.

I finished the paperwork I had to complete and changed into jeans in the staff room so I wasn't in my work pants again.

I had a few questions for my beautiful males and I needed answers. How was this strange relationship supposed to work? There were two of them and only one of me.

Would I always be enough for them?

What if Brandon decided he was going to date on the side, or something stupid like that?

Acid burned in my belly at the thought and I swallowed against the sick sensation swelling like a wave as it approached the shore. I wouldn't be able to handle anything other than full exclusivity. From both of them.

I said goodnight to my staff and traveled the twenty minutes to my men's home, then walked up to the front door with butterflies the size of cats flying around in my tummy.

The door opened before I had the chance to knock on the intricately carved timber.

"Oh, hi!"

Tyler reached out and pulled me into the warmth of his arms.

I laughed against his lips as he tilted me off-balance. His strong arms held me as he showered my face with kisses. "Hello to you, too," I managed.

He chuckled and planted one more quick kiss on my lips before he kicked the door shut and brought me down the hallway and into the huge living area where Brandon sat on the couch.

"You hungry, babe?" My blond lover spoke up from his comfortable perch. I moved away from Tyler to greet him, throwing my leg over Brandon's lap and straddling him.

Normally I'd worry I was too fat to do this, but my men were supernaturally strong. They'd already proven that.

"No, not yet." I leaned forward to kiss him, our lips meeting and heat building between us.

When he stood up, I was still wrapped around him.

I opened my eyes when he pulled back from the kiss to see his eyes flicker to lion-yellow. I slid down his body and my feet landed on the floor. Was that flicker his lion shifter?

"I need to talk to you guys about something."

Tyler moved over and pulled me down onto his lap and Brandon continued to sit sideways with his eyes fixed on my face.

"Sure, babe, what's up?" Tyler ran his fingertips down my arms, making me relax and sink into his strong embrace.

I bit my lip and looked between my two gorgeous men. How was this discussion going to progress? I was loathe to throw any tension into our newfound happiness, but this had to be raised.

I took a breath and relaxed into Tyler's arms, looking at my blond-haired god across the room. *Here goes...*

"How's this going to work exactly?"

Brandon cocked his head and raised an eyebrow. "What do you mean?"

I inhaled through my nose, then let it out again. I didn't want to have to spell it out, but these were men. Subtlety wasn't going to work.

"Are you two going to be faithful to me? Or does monogamy not exist in this kind of relationship?"

Tyler chuckled, his chest vibrating the way a cat's does when it purrs.

Funny, that.

Brandon gave me a weird look with a smile flirting around the edges of his strong mouth. "Why, Laura? I hope you're not asking if it's okay for you to see other men."

I stared at Brandon, then burst out laughing when I saw the smile turn into a frown. "You're kidding me. You guys are more than enough for me!"

Brandon's tight shoulders relaxed. "Why ask then?"

I grimaced, hating the weakness within me, and my logical brain that screamed at me for my hypocrisy.

"Because, technically, I'm not being monogamous. I have both of you, and you only have me. I'd love to say you could have someone else if you really wanted to, but I think it would break my heart if you slept with someone else." *There! I said it.*

Tyler chuckled again, wrapping his arms around my waist and squeezing hard. "Of course, we'll commit to only you, Laura. I certainly don't want anyone else, and as far as the monogamy thing goes, you will be faithful—and that's more important. Just to two men, not one."

Tyler kissed my temple, the gesture sending warm honey through to my core.

I glanced across the room and could almost *see* the internal struggle going on in Brandon's head. His face was twisted into a weird expression.

"You okay?" I asked, attempting to rise to go to him, yet Tyler held me tight.

Brandon shrugged. "Yeah, I'm fine. I hadn't really thought about it."

I swallowed, fear fluttering in my belly. "Which part? About you being monogamous? Or the hypocrisy of me expecting it, when I'm not really giving it?"

Brandon nodded, and his eyes took on a glazed sort of look.

Oh God, it's going to kill me if he doesn't want to be monogamous.

I hurried on. "If you aren't ready for this, Brandon, I understand. I don't think I can choose between you, but if you aren't comfortable, or want some more time to enjoy being single, maybe I can stay with Tyler and you can—"

"No!" The word shot out into the room, silencing anything else I would have said.

Brandon sat up straighter in his chair and flicked his head at me. "Come here."

Tyler released me and helped me to my feet.

I walked over to my big Viking, my legs trembling with each step. He grabbed me and pulled me down into his lap as soon as I was within reach, his solid bulk supporting me and making me feel safe and small.

"I've never been monogamous before. I've liked the freedom of being able to do whatever, and with whoever, I want."

I struggled to get off Brandon's lap, anger filling me up so quickly I could see red flashing in my vision as I growled.

Brandon's arms clamped down and I struck out at him, my futile attempts to get away making tears spring to my eyes. "Then let me go! If you don't want me, I'll leave."

A wounded noise sounded behind me and I ignored it. Tyler wouldn't like the idea of me leaving, but I couldn't stay if it meant Brandon kept sleeping around. "Stop it, silly woman. That's not what I meant. Now, let me finish."

Brandon was squashing me into his chest and holding my arms down so I was tucked into him. His heart beat loudly under me and I found the sound soothing as I settled to press my ear against his chest.

As my anger drained away, I closed my eyes and nestled in, finding the most comfortable spot where all of my body was warm and caressed.

"What *did* you mean, then?"

He sighed and squeezed me again. "I mean...I will commit to you, only to you. I don't care about Tyler being there, too, that's not an issue in our community. I have always known I'd share a mate with my brother, I don't think of it as cheating."

A huge weight lifted off my shoulders and I sagged heavier into Brandon's embrace. Now that my anger had gone, I was left feeling vulnerable and a little fragile, and open to whatever feelings and thoughts they wished to share. "So, what is it then?"

Brandon groaned and shifted me so that my ass was right over his crotch. I wiggled because I couldn't resist and he squeezed me again.

Brandon sighed. "Just remember that this is new for me. I'm not used to it yet."

I had to ask. "Do you want anyone else?"

Silence for a moment, then Brandon barked out a laugh. "No. I don't. I had a woman proposition me this morning at the gym and I growled at her. I wasn't even slightly interested, though she was hot, and that's strange for me. I'm not sure I entirely like the feeling."

I ignored the *she was hot* comment because it had way too many squigglies in it for me, and processed the rest of the information.

There'd always be good-looking women around. The concern was whether or not my men found them tempting.

So, the problem was that the big, wild cat wasn't interested in all the other pussies anymore? And he was... worried? He probably thought something was wrong with him.

I slipped my hands under Brandon's t-shirt and teased his tight little nipples with my fingers. "*I* like the feeling." I began gyrating on his lap, rubbing my pussy against his rising cock, and loving the feel of the feminine power. "I love the fact you want me above all others."

Brandon grunted, though I wasn't sure whether or not it was in agreement with my assumption. I raised my head to stare into his blue eyes and found them strangely cautious-looking.

I smiled up at him with as much warmth as possible. "Because I need you."

Brandon crushed me against him and kissed me, his hunger evident in the thrust of his tongue into my mouth and the way his hands clung to my body like a dying man in need of my love.

LAURA

15

I stepped into the noisy bar with my men. The smell of sweat and beer assaulted my nostrils, yet I giggled like a schoolgirl on my first date.

I felt so special standing there. Brandon and Tyler's protective postures resembled strutting peacocks and angry gorillas all in one.

Some huge guy stood in front of us grinning like he'd won something, his muscular build very similar to Brandon's.

"Hey, Ty. Brandon. Who's your friend?"

I waited to see what they would do and was surprised when Brandon spoke up. "Jim, this is Laura. Laura... Jim, a friend of mine from work."

Brandon's mouth was turned down and he was shifting from foot to foot, as though readying himself for a fight.

Calm down, honey.

"Hey." I nodded at the guy.

Jim stepped forward with a slight leer. "Wanna' dance?"

I laughed at the offer. This wasn't exactly the sort of place I'd want to dance with a stranger. Brandon stepped in front of me, blocking Jim's advance as effectively as a solar eclipse. "I don't think so."

I turned to my right when a feminine hand slid into mine. I turned to face a gorgeous redhead rolling her eyes in Brandon's direction.

"Hey, Renee." I greeted the twins' sister with relief. Hopefully her presence would defuse the situation if it started to get out of hand.

"Hi, Laura, let's get a drink." Renee tugged me away from the boys and I let her. Why not? May as well get to know the sister of the men I was probably going to spend the rest of my life with.

I watched with amusement as Tyler and Brandon's mouths dropped open, looking more like cartoon characters than the big men they were.

"I can't believe they're so protective." I nodded at Tyler and Brandon, and Renee laughed with a gusto similar to her brothers.

"You're kidding. They're men who've found the only woman designed for them. They're not leaving anything to chance."

Holy hell, that sounds intense!

"What can I get you to drink?" the bartender asked us, and I swung around on my seat, facing the cute guy and giving him an automatic smile.

"Renee?" I turned to the woman who had befriended me last Sunday before she'd known a thing about me.

"Yeah. Whiskey for me."

I grimaced. "Yuck. Red wine for me, please."

A hand pushed some money across the bar and I looked up to see Tyler paying for our drinks.

"Thanks, sweetie."

Tyler dropped his head and planted a kiss on my lips. It was hard, possessive and very thorough. I threaded my hands through his hair and held him tightly as white light tingled around my brain.

When he finally lifted his head, his expression was soft. "You okay?"

I nodded. "Of course. You go talk to your friends. I'll hang with Renee for a bit."

Tyler glanced over to the corner where Brandon was standing with a group of guys. "Okay, but come find me as soon as you want."

He kissed me once more and swaggered over to cheers by the group.

"What was that about?" I indicated to the men, who were handing beers around.

Renee laughed. "Tyler's been sulking for months now. His friends will give him a bit of crap tonight about that little display, but don't worry. They're happy for him and Brandon."

I frowned, watching the back-slapping and beer-guzzling with a jaded eye. "Is this what every Saturday night is going to be like from now on, then?"

Renee handed me a glass of red wine and we clinked our glasses together. "Cheers, and to answer your question, no. I have a feeling this may be one of the last times you'll be here. The boys are too in love with you to take you to places like this."

I was forever grateful I hadn't been actually *drinking* my wine when Renee said such a thing. I would have sprayed my drink all over the gorgeous woman in front of me if I had. "Did you just say 'in love with me'?"

Renee could *not* mean that.

"Yeah, of course." Renee grinned and tossed back her whiskey, swallowing it in one smooth motion.

"But...it's only been a week!" This made no sense whatsoever.

"Shifters are like that. Mate for life, Fated soul mates. Blah, blah, blah."

Heat seared my cheeks and she looked away for a moment. I was still finding it a little hard dealing with the whole, *men-who-turn-into-mountain-lions* thing, but Renee, of course, had been dealing with it her entire life.

"Nae!"

"Rosie!" Renee waved at a cute blonde woman across the bar. "Do you mind if I run over to chat with Rosie for a minute?"

I waved her off. "Go, go. I'm going to enjoy my wine and think."

Renee winked and jumped up, her sexy little bum sashaying away. I would have been jealous of Renee's physique once upon a time. But Tyler and Brandon had satisfied me so completely, making love to me in every way I knew, and ways I'd never dreamed of.

Why should I be worried?

"So... you're the new girl Tyler's screwing?"

I swiveled on my stool, gaping at the woman sneering at me. Was she really talking to me? "Excuse me?"

I stared at the woman in front of me. This could *not* be the sort of bed partner Tyler usually went for. She was dark and short, attractive in a skanky sort of way. But her aura was horrible, all ice and flint.

The woman tossed her head like a horse. "Tyler and his brother have slept with most of the women in this bar. I wanted to warn you not to get too attached."

Another woman, this one tall and blonde, stepped up beside the dark one.

"Yeah, you know you won't last, right? Those two never keep any woman around for more than a week or two."

I swallowed the burning in my throat and tried not to think about my lovers taking these women into their beds. "Why are you talking to me?"

The dark one nodded. "You should be warned. You look like a nice chick. They take you to their beds, make you feel loved, act like you're special and shit. I mean, boy, do they know how to screw, right?"

Acid burned in my tummy and I placed the wineglass down with shaking hands.

"Do they now? How would you know? Had both of them, have you?"

The blonde narrowed her eyes at me. "They never cross swords. I slept with Brandon a few weeks ago, and he told me his brother and he never share."

A small flame of triumph flared in my belly, despite the anger and jealousy threatening to consume me. My heart was pounding and I could barely swallow the bile rising in my throat. This was a nightmare come true.

I gathered my courage and pushed forward. "Well, I'm glad you weren't good enough for both of them. But I am."

The women reeled back as though I'd struck them.

"What?" The blonde gasped. "You're screwing *both* of them?"

I shuddered at the word, unable to link the two images together —the way my men touched me—loved me—and the crude way these women were talking about it.

These women had shared the same things with Brandon and Tyler as I had? Impossible.

"No. I make love to them."

The woman began to laugh, a cackling, evil sound. "You're kidding, right? Those boys fuck anything with tits and a cunt. They may talk sweet, but they don't even remember your name when they're fucking you all night long."

The girls around me continued to laugh with cruel intent and I was back in high school again. The butt of everyone's jokes.

I was going to be sick.

Visions of my men doing those things to me flashed before my eyes.

Heat bloomed in my cheeks and I gripped the bar so I didn't topple off my seat.

Another woman came along and the dark one grabbed her.

"This is Tyler's new chick."

The new one, who had beautiful eyes, smirked. "Lucky bitch. Enjoy him while you can. He has the most talented tongue. I've tried to get back in with him for another go, but he likes new flesh."

The beautiful eyes looked me up and down, showing her true colors as the ugliness surged, transforming her once-pretty face. "And there's plenty of you to go around, so you might last longer than us."

I was really going to be sick now. My stomach surged and I jumped up. "I have to go."

I pushed through the group of women, their laughter following me as I made my way to the bathroom. I burst into the dirty little room and locked myself in a stall, shaking uncontrollably as hot tears rolled down my face.

How many historical romance novels had I read that professed that the best men to love were reformed rakes?

A bad boy who turned good just for you?

It so wasn't true. *Damn it.* Loving men like that hurt.

The sobbing started and I covered my mouth with my hand, rocking back and forth. I couldn't compete with women like that! I didn't *want* to. How could I ever believe that they'd stay with me, if those were the sort of women they liked.

I unrolled some toilet paper and wiped at my face, memories of our times together flashing in my mind like a porn movie. I'd believed them when they said I was special.

But I wasn't.

I was just one of the many women they'd fucked and the first they'd tried sharing.

How many women had they licked?

How many vaginas had those cocks been in?

I'd sucked them and loved every minute of it. How could I make love to them now that I knew what sort of men they were?

Whores. Both of them.

I took a deep, shuddering breath as a group of girls burst into the bathroom. I needed to get home—*now*, where I could be alone. I stood up on shaky legs, making sure my breathing was at least a little regular, then I stepped out into the room.

The women all stared at me, one little redhead stepping close. "You okay?"

I nodded, walking to the mirror and inspecting the damage. *Crap.* Thank God I didn't wear much makeup.

I turned to the woman who'd showed me some empathy. "I need to get out of here, but don't have my car. Are there any cabs out front?"

The redhead lay a gentle hand on my arm. "No, I'd call an Uber if you have an account."

"Oh yeah." My sister had set that up on my phone ages ago, I'd just never used it. "I don't usually..."

The red head took my phone, tapped a few buttons and smiled.

"They're only a few minutes away, so when you go out of here, just turn left and follow the hallway. It'll take you right to the front where the Uber will be waiting."

"Thank you so much." I took my phone back and checked my pockets. I still had money. Perfect.

I was so done living in this fantasy world. Better to get out now before I got my heart totally shattered.

"Thanks." I nodded at the one kind woman I'd met tonight and ducked out the door.

Unfortunately, I ran straight into a gorgeous, skinny, platinum-blonde.

"Look who we have here. You're Laura, aren't you?"

I nodded, defeated. What more could be said tonight?

"Well, I'm Simone."

The woman placed her hand on her hip, the tone of her voice making it clear that she thought she was important.

"Yeah, so?"

Simone glared at me, fire spitting out of her ugly aura. "You know Brandon left you to come to me last night?"

What?!

White noise filled my head as the breath froze in my lungs. "What are you talking about?"

The blonde tossed her glistening long hair over her shoulder. "Brandon was in my bed last night. I know you think you have them all to yourself, but you don't. They'll always find a way to get what they need, and you obviously can't give it to them."

Pain shot through my chest. A piercing, crippling sensation that had me staggering back and fumbling along the wall toward the back door.

This *wasn't* happening.

I should have listened to my inner voice when it had told me this was all too good to be true.

My phone vibrated in my pocket, and it made me move faster. My men were too smooth-tongued for me to trust them to tell the truth.

I fell out the back door and into the cold night air. A white Uber waited by the curb and I stumbled toward it. I yanked open the door and told the man my address.

My swollen eyelids slid down over my painfully gritty eyes and I wrapped my arms around my shaking body.

I felt cold, empty, and disgusting. Had I left a part of my soul back in that bar?

As the silence fell on me like a brick wall, I knew I'd have to face the truth. I'd already fallen in love with Tyler and Brandon, and without them I'd live my life with half my soul missing.

Tyler

I walked to the back of the darkened bar again and looked over to where Renee stood by the bar. She lifted her arms in a confused shrug and I briefly closed my eyes.

What the hell had happened?

One minute I'd been drinking beer with some buddies and the next thing I knew, our woman was missing. I made my way back to Renee in time to meet up with Brandon, who'd been doing another lap outside.

"One of the bouncers said she left about half an hour ago."

"What?" I couldn't believe it. "Why would she do that?"

I turned to my sister. "Nae, what did you say to her?"

Renee held up her hands and stepped back as though she'd been struck. "Nothing, I swear. Although, I probably shouldn't have left her alone for so long. I did see a couple of women talking to her, but I didn't think much of it."

I shuddered as an ex of mine walked past and gave me fluttery eyes.

I looked away with a grimace. "Did we do something totally moronic bringing her here?" I asked Brandon, a feeling of cold dread slithering up my spine and circling my chest.

"I'm gonna call her again."

"No. You've already called her ten times." I thought quickly. *What to do?*

"Let's drive over to her place. If the lights are on, we'll bang on the door, and if they're not, we'll go back in the morning."

Brandon grunted his agreement and we headed toward the door.

Twenty minutes later, we were sitting in the car outside Laura's house, staring at the bricks and mortar.

"No lights on. I'll call her again."

I let Brandon do whatever he wanted, but I knew she wouldn't pick up the phone. Something was wrong.

"Pick up, pick up, pick up," Brandon chanted, tapping his foot on the floor of the car.

I shook my head and turned the car back on. "Let's get some sleep. Tomorrow is going to be a very long, interesting day."

We drove home in silence, my head buzzing with recriminations while my heart sank lower into my chest.

What if we'd lost her forever?

I wouldn't be able to live.

I wouldn't want to.

LAURA

16

Someone was pounding on my front door, and my cell phone was vibrating its little heart away on the coffee table. It was barely eight a.m. and I didn't need three guesses to know who was behind both.

I closed my eyes and picked up the remote control to turn on the TV. Loud.

"Laura, we know you're in there. Please open the door and tell us what's wrong. Did something happen last night?"

Tyler's voice was calm, but I could hear the strain behind it.

"Go away!" I shouted through my front door before whispering, "Please, just leave me alone."

I didn't want to do this.

Bang, bang, bang. A bigger fist this time.

"Laura!"

I shivered at the growl behind Brandon's words. I half expected him to ram the door, which I wouldn't deny he probably had the strength to do. Squeezing my eyes shut, I realized I was going to have to let them in before they did some damage to either themselves or the door.

I didn't want to, but at least we could have it out once and for all.

I stalked to the front door, took a deep breath, and wrenched it open.

On my doorstep stood my two powerful men, my night and day,

the moon and the stars of my world... and at least one was a bloody cheating bastard.

"I have nothing to say to either of you. We're done, and I don't want to see you again."

Brandon's eyes grew impossibly wide and Tyler actually put a hand over his heart as though I'd shot him with a bullet to the heart.

I tapped my foot, then threw my hands in the air. They looked pathetic standing out there. "Fine, come in!"

I stomped into my living area and stood in the middle of what had previously always felt like a cozy room, but now felt like a tin can.

I crossed my arms over my chest and waited.

The men walked in and Tyler came at me first, his gentle eyes pleading with me. "Sweetheart, I don't know what's going on. We were at the bar having a great time and you disappeared. We've been calling you all night."

I knew that. They'd left dozens of messages that I'd snuck peeks at through my long night alone. I'd ended up switching my cell off and sobbing through the remaining hours of darkness. "I know, and I'm sorry I ran out on you, but I couldn't cope with that... black hole of sluttiness."

Brandon leaned back against the wall and crossed his arms.

Tyler walked closer. "Was it because we left you alone, beautiful girl? Brandon and I shouldn't have taken you to a place like that. You're better than that."

I laughed—what else could I do? But even to my own ears the sound was bitter and almost cruel. "Yeah, I am way better than that. But for future reference, it's never a good move to take your girlfriend out, then abandon her—but that's not the point. Get out, both of you."

I pointed at the front door and glared at my men, the men I loved with all my heart, the men I thought would always protect me, care for me, and love me. Where had they been last night when I was attacked by all those bitchy women?

"Laura, I don't know what's happened." Tyler, my beautiful, sweet man stepped forward again so that he was within arm's reach.

I backed up three feet.

"Ask your brother." I threw a dirty look at Brandon and watched as shock registered on his handsome face.

"Me? What'd I do?"

I groaned. "I know you were with Simone Friday night. She told me. I heard nothing but stories about you guys all night. The women you've slept with, the legions of broken hearts you've left behind."

Brandon growled a little, the sound causing the hairs on my arms to stand up. "What? Simone? I was *not* with her."

"Then where were you?" I shot back. "You didn't get home until three a.m." I remembered because I'd woken up when he slid back into bed and I'd looked at the clock.

"I was running. I shifted after dinner and needed to get out."

Really? That's the best excuse you can come up with?

"Bullshit. You've fought this three-way mating thing from the start. I know you don't really want me, or the commitment I need."

Brandon began to shake his head, hissing angrily as he paced my wooden floors.

I waited for him to correct my arrogant presumption, but he didn't.

I knew it.

"And you!" I rounded on Tyler. "Every woman in that bar knew what you were like in bed, especially how much you love to lick pussy! Oh my God, if I had to hear once more how amazing your tongue is... Did you leave a single ass unturned, or were you trying to break some sort of record?"

Tyler's mouth fell open and he gaped like a fish.

Didn't these idiots have any idea what women were like?

Could they even comprehend what it felt like for me? To know that my men had groped a hundred women the same way they'd touched me.

It made me feel dirty, common, and completely unloved.

"Like I said, get out!"

"Laura, you've got it all wrong," Tyler said.

Me? Me!

Heat and pain exploded inside my head as angry tears gathered and slid down my face. "Get out! Get out! Get out!"

I marched over to the front door and threw it open. My heart was hammering in my chest and I was struggling to breathe.

The men finally moved, dragging their feet like school boys who didn't want to go. Tyler looked hurt and lost, while Brandon was making wild cat noises and prancing like he was near a female in heat.

As soon as they'd both stepped over my threshold once again, I slammed the door and slid home the bolt, collapsing on the floor in massive, heartbreaking sobs.

Didn't they understand?

What had I done wrong to deserve such treatment?

And after Brandon had promised me—*promised*—that I was enough.

I wrapped my arms around my knees and tucked myself into a ball.

I had no fight left in me, and the misery consumed me. Hot, salty tears rolled down my face, choking me and making me gasp and wheeze.

I would never get over this. I could never make love to them the same way as before. Not now.

How could I kiss their lips, feel their hands against me, take them inside my body and my heart, knowing that none of it was special to them?

I stayed on the floor until my ass was numb and I was utterly exhausted, then I rolled onto my side and fell asleep.

It was Sunday, my one day off each week. Belle had stayed over at a friend's house and I had no responsibilities for a few hours.

There was no need to get up off the floor. Even to stagger to my bed.

~

BRANDON

Tyler glared at me. "Brandon, I swear to God, if you've screwed this up for us..."

"That fucking bitch Simone lied!" I roared at Tyler as we ran to his car and threw open the door. *That stupid, lying skank!*

I could feel my mountain lion rising like a flood. Heat prickled my skin and my eyes shifted so that my sight was clearer and more distinct than a human's would be.

I pressed down into my gut with my diaphragm and exhaled. I didn't know if I could hold my shifter back, but I had to try.

"Shit!" I roared. We weren't in a safe place. And it was hunting season. I didn't even know the quickest way to the mountains from here.

"Brandon. Look at me, brother."

I forced my gaze back to Tyler, who was staring hard. It gave me something to focus on while I pushed my animal down, holding on to my humanity by the proverbial skin of my teeth.

"We can fix this. I know we can. You weren't really with Simone Friday night, were you?"

I growled and shook my head, panting and pacing alongside the car.

"No, of course not! I tossed her aside months ago. Fucking her was like screwing a cadaver."

I shuddered as my mind conjured up memories of Simone. Like most of my lovers, she expected me to do everything. As a general rule, I didn't mind since I loved sex, but she gave *nothing* back. I got sick of it months before I'd even met Laura. I'd found it hard work keeping my cock stiff when she did nothing but lie there and use me like a dildo with hands.

Not that I'd ever admitted that to anyone.

"Then why did she say you were?" Tyler asked quietly.

I took a deep, calming breath and let it out slowly, not sure how or why the woman would do such a thing. Jealousy, probably. Or spite. Who the fuck knew why some women did what they did?

"Because she's a bitch."

Tyler frowned, obviously not happy with that answer.

"I don't have a better answer for you, Ty. Simone has nothing to gain from breaking us all up."

Tyler's eyes widened and his face turned a sickly pale gray. "Hang on. Did Laura just break up with us?"

I growled. "Yeah. She did."

Tyler wheezed next to me. "Wait. I...she can't do that."

I agreed. And yet she had. We were meant to be together. Sure, I'd fought it a bit. Who wouldn't when he was losing his carefree lifestyle basically overnight? But that didn't mean I didn't want her. Flushes of pain crashed over me in waves.

I stopped pacing and stared at the house, where I could still hear sniffling noises coming through the door. She was crying, the silly woman.

"What the fuck do we do?" I said. "We can't leave her like that."

I pointed toward the house, glaring hard. Part of me didn't want to go in and deal with her tears; they'd break my heart. But another part wanted to rush right in and scoop her up into my arms. I wanted to comfort her. Protect her from pain. Standing out here feeling impotent and lost was like torture.

Tyler looked back over his shoulder, then opened the car door.

"We'll make it worse, Brandon. We're in way above our head here."

My baby brother slid into the car and I followed suit, a massive pain in my chest blossoming over the anger and hurt consuming me.

I couldn't breathe right.

"Let's go." Tyler's voice was firm and authoritative, which was perfect because I could not have found my way out of a paper bag at the moment.

"Where are we going?" I asked as Tyler pulled the car onto the road and headed out of Hinton.

"Mom and Dad's. They'll know what to do."

I groaned but did what I was told. My head was clearing now. At least we had a plan of attack.

"You sure about that? Mom's always looked down on us for partying the way we have in the past. She may be on Laura's side."

Tyler sighed and shifted in the chair next to him. "Yeah, I know. But if there's anyone who can help, our family can."

We stayed quiet for the rest of the car ride before finally pulling up in front of our family home.

I sighed and dragged myself out of the car, my chest still aching like I'd been run through with a knife.

Laura

Loud banging on my front door made me jump, then an urgent female voice broke through my cloud of misery as I stared at the bright computer screen in front of me. I'd been trying to do some research for a much-needed vacation. "Laura! Help us! Please!"

I ran to the front door, my heart pumping wildly as I wrenched it open. There was Renee, her face pale and streaked with tears.

"What is it? What's happened?" I looked across the lawn and saw Brandon and practically his whole family parked outside my house, an old pickup I hadn't seen before parked behind my car.

Renee grabbed my hand. "Tyler's been shot!"

No!

Adrenaline surged at her words and I bolted across the lawn, headless of my bare feet and no bra. I grabbed hold of the side rails of the pickup truck and stared down into the bed.

Brandon held a magnificent mountain lion in his arms while

Rosalie pressed white gauze to the side of the animal. His golden fur and black-tipped ears were perfect. But the blood seeping from his side sent my thoughts into a tailspin.

"He can't shift back, or he'll die. Please." Rosalie's voice cracked with pain and tears rolled down her puffy cheeks. "Help him."

Autopilot settled in and a stillness crept over me, calming my muscles and heart. "I need to get the clinic keys, then you guys can follow me there. I don't have the necessary equipment here to operate."

I didn't wait for a response. I turned and fled, quickly grabbing shoes and keys before bolting to my car. "Renee! With me!" I called out.

I was more grateful than I could express when the redhead jumped into the passenger side of my car without question and we took off. "Tell me what happened."

"Well, I only got there after Ty had taken off, but from what I was told the boys came to Mom and Dad for help with how to win you back, and Ty got so upset he shifted and ran off."

I nodded, but refused to allow my heart to register anything but the bare facts. Now was not the time to get emotional. Blame would be waiting for me later, like luggage left at the bottom of the stairs after a holiday.

"Go on."

"When he didn't come back, Brandon and Dad shifted and took off to find him, only to return carrying him. It's hunting season out there and we're usually extra careful at this time of year. He'd been shot by some hunter and was barely breathing. Mom knows enough first aid to patch us up when we get injured, but she didn't want to even try this time. Not with a bullet wound. We just loaded him up and came straight to you."

I swung my car into the clinic parking lot and turned off the engine.

Maybe I should invest in a mobile clinic at home.

"She did the right thing. Let's go."

I stepped out, feeling the panic washing away in front of the clinic's imposing façade. This was my domain, and if anyone could save him, I could.

I unlocked the door and moved into the staff room with short, sharp moves, tying up my hair and pulling on a clean scrub top.

I opened all the doors and began ushering people through like a traffic director. "In here, on the operating table. I need two sets of hands, preferably Renee and Rosalie. The rest of you, wait somewhere else."

I really should call one of my vet techs in, but the last thing I wanted to do was expose Tyler or any of his family to the local community. There was probably some shifter law about that.

I turned back to the sink to wash my hands and focused on nothing but my knowledge of mountain lion anatomy. They weren't too different from any other large cat, but this wasn't just a normal four-legged feline.

Tyler's mine.

I shook my head to clear the thought. No point in thinking too vividly about who was lying on the table. "Renee, is there any special physiology that I need to know about? Being a shifter? Or can I treat Tyler like a normal mountain lion in this form?"

I turned back to the room, now empty of all the men except for the patient lying still on the table.

Renee shook her head and lay her hand on Tyler's hind legs while Rosalie stroked his head and murmured to him.

"No, I don't think so. Mom?"

Rosalie shook her head, tears beginning to leak down her cheeks once again.

"Okay. I'll need to remove the bullet and repair any damage it's caused. I'll gas him to keep him unconscious while I operate, and give him some painkillers and antibiotics when he wakes up."

Both women stood straighter and nodded, seemingly gaining strength from the straightforward instructions. I pulled over a silver tray of newly disinfected instruments and set up the anesthetic gas.

I set the dial and reached down to attach it to Tyler's snout. I had assumed he was already unconscious, but he groaned softly as I lifted his head.

"Tyler, if you can hear me, I want you to know that you have to stay strong and survive this. Okay? Do you understand? I'm still mad at you and if you die, you won't be able to make it up to me."

A strange purring noise came from his chest and Rosalie burst into tears.

Pain shot through my heart and I pushed it down, away, to deal with later.

I settled the mask onto my precious patient and stroked his head with my fingers. "Sleep well, beautiful boy."

Tyler's body began to relax and I pinned the two women opposite me with the hardest stare I could muster.

"Listen, I can handle this on my own if I have to. If you can't be in here, I totally understand. But I need your undivided attention and concentration if you're staying."

Rosalie started to back toward the door. "I don't think I..."

I smiled at the beautiful mother who could barely look as her baby went under the knife.

"I understand, Rosalie. Now, close the door behind you, and Renee and I will be out when I'm done. An hour, maybe more."

Rosalie nodded and disappeared and I turned to Tyler's sister. "You okay with this? There's going to be a lot of blood."

Renee stalked over to the sink and began scrubbing her hands. "I've seen more of Tyler and Brandon's blood over the years than I care to mention."

Water ran in the sink and Renee finally turned back, her green eyes hard. "Where do you want me?"

I smiled my approval at her attitude, and pointed to the top of the table. "Here. Watch his breathing, make sure the mask stays in place, and hand me items when I ask for them."

I carefully shaved around the wound area so that his fur wouldn't interfere with the surgery, then set the clippers down.

Oh, God. This is Tyler*!*

It's okay. You can do this.

I took a deep, steadying breath, picked up the scalpel, and set it to the bloody mess that had once been Tyler's beautiful shoulder.

"All right. Here we go..."

BRANDON

17

I paced the floor back and forth so many times my feet ached, and if I looked down I'd probably see the path I'd worn in the clinic waiting room. "What the hell's taking so long?"

My mother sniffed and lifted her wrist to look at her watch for the hundredth time.

"It's only been forty-three minutes and she said an hour. That bullet could have gotten lodged anywhere. If Tyler dies because of something I said..."

I tossed up my hands and made a disgusted noise in my mother's direction.

"Mom! If there's anyone to blame, you know it's fucking me! Or fucking Tyler! Seriously? He's never learned to control his mountain lion, and just because Laura dumped us doesn't mean he had to go running off into the woods in the middle of the day. During hunting season! How stupid can he be?"

My parents' eyes shifted to the space behind me. I whirled to see Laura standing in the doorway, blood covering her scrubs and her shoulder keeping the door open. "Tyler's in recovery."

"Is he going to be all right?" I asked, swallowing the lump that had risen when I saw the woman who was meant to be our mate standing there.

Laura nodded and straightened, that strength I admired shining through.

"I'm going to clean up and then I'll come back out. I just wanted to tell you right away that he's alive and doing well."

She turned and disappeared back into the surgical area and my heart began to thud with sickening, slow thumps. My knees weakened and I staggered to one of those flimsy white chairs and crashed down into it.

Renee came bolting through the door, her eyes wide and a little crazy.

"Oh my God, she is amazing! *I'm* in love with her! How did she do that? I have no idea! All *with* knowing it was *Tyler* on the table. I would have been a complete mess."

Words were flying out of Renee's mouth so fast I wasn't quite keeping up. My adrenaline had run out of steam, but it was pretty obvious my sister was still high on the rush.

I blinked and took a deep breath, hoping to stop the rapid whirl of stress washing through my body. My head was spinning.

"Did she get the bullet out?" Dad asked, taking Renee by the hand to calm her down.

"Yeah, but it was touch and go for a while. The bullet was lodged in some plexus where all the nerves and blood vessels go. I didn't really understand what she was saying. But she got it out without too much blood loss. She is so amazing!"

Renee squealed and I dropped my head into my hands. Touch and go? My brother could have *died*? I gulped air as heated emotions swamped me.

"You fucking idiot." Tears dripped down my face and, angrily, I wiped them away. I wasn't sure who I was talking to—probably myself.

Laura walked into the waiting room once again and I shot to my feet, my need to touch her scary in its intensity. My fingers itched to reach out and my cock twitched in my pants.

I needed to claim that woman before she got more silly notions in her head. Once we were mated, the connection between us would be too strong to ever break.

"Tyler needs to stay here overnight, and I'm going to stay with him. Then we can transport him home tomorrow and I'm happy to move into the house for a few days to look after him if that's okay with you all?" She speared me with a questioning look.

My cock twitched again. *Yes, that is a very good plan.*

"He'll need consistent monitoring and I don't think it's safe to keep him here in case he suddenly shifts back to human," she added.

She stared at me, and if she was trying to communicate something, I didn't understand what it was. "*Is* that okay with you, Brandon?"

I realized I hadn't answered and I quickly nodded, clearing my throat before speaking. "Absolutely. That sounds great. Thank you."

Laura looked back at Mom, and for the first time I saw the pallor in my mate's cheeks, the slump to her shoulders. Maybe she hadn't handled that surgery as well as she said she did.

"When will he be able to shift back, Rosalie?"

His mother shrugged. "I'm not sure. As soon as he's strong enough. A day, two, maybe. Shifters heal very quickly."

Laura's shoulders sagged even further and the protector in me took over.

"Laura, get your tech to watch Tyler tonight and you can come home with me. You're exhausted."

Laura's eyes widened and she shook her head with a grim frown. "No, if something goes wrong, I need to be here."

I walked over to our woman and took her hand. "I'll pay for someone. Bring in whoever you want, or your partner, if you think that's a better choice. And tomorrow we'll both come back here together to take him home. You need sleep."

I leaned forward, my heart in my throat as I whispered into Laura's ear. The woman who had broken up with me this morning and then saved Tyler's life this afternoon.

"Come home with me, baby girl. Please."

Laura pulled back abruptly and stared at me, her eyes shadowed with worry and shiny with tears. She didn't actually speak, but I took her silence for acquiescence. "Do you need to make some phone calls?"

Laura nodded slowly, a tear sliding down her cheek that she quickly swiped away.

"All right, I'll wait for you."

I squeezed her hand and stepped away, my mountain lion raising his head and growling at the idea of leaving her.

We're taking her with us. Don't worry.

I headed back over to my parents. I'd never really identified my mountain lion as a separate part of myself, but today I was talking to the shifter for the first time like he was.

"Laura's going to call someone else to come in and watch Tyler overnight, and she'll come home with me for some rest."

Dad smiled knowingly and Mom clung to his arm. "Should I stay? I could sleep here overnight."

Laura joined us, standing by my side with her back straight and strong. My lion purred with pride as she spoke. "No, Rosalie, I think we all need to go home and have a break. The other vet is coming in and she will call me if anything goes wrong. I'll stay at my house so that I'm closer to Tyler if I do need to come back during the night."

I didn't care where she wanted to sleep, but I'd be right beside her all night, keeping both of our nightmares away.

"Mom, Dad, take Nae home and we'll see you guys tomorrow."

We waved my parents off and I took Laura into my arms, not caring when she was stiff and unresponsive. We had a few things to work out. "Go get organized and I'll wait for you here."

I leaned forward and kissed her, not sure if she'd turn away, but not caring either. When our lips connected, I moaned and pulled her closer. Laura's hands gently touched my face before we pulled apart.

"Ah... I'll go call Claire. I'd prefer not to go home with you, if that's all right?"

She looked away and I shrugged.

"Your place... mine, I don't care. I've gotta make a few phone calls too, so you'll let me know when it's time to go home?"

Laura stared at me again with that searching look that made me wonder how she was *really* feeling. During the week, we'd forged a connection that had surpassed anything I'd ever experienced or felt.

Then, in one night—half an hour—we'd lost her. It seemed impossible.

I didn't understand and she certainly didn't seem inclined to explain, either.

Laura finally nodded once and headed into the clinic.

I pulled out my phone and called my boss to let him know I had a personal emergency and needed the week off. I would find out exactly what had gone wrong with Laura. And then I would fix it.

18

I CHECKED ON TYLER ONCE MORE, THEN HEARD THE FRONT DOOR OPEN AND close.

"Laura, its Claire."

I bent down and kissed Tyler's head, closing my eyes for a moment to inhale his scent. "I'll see you tomorrow."

I'd never operated on a boyfriend before... *but I suppose there's a first time for everything.*

I headed out into the waiting room and smiled at the woman whose skill I trusted almost as much as my own. "Thanks so much for coming in, Claire. I removed a bullet from a mountain lion's shoulder a few hours ago and I need you to monitor him overnight."

Claire's eyes widened with shock. "You have a mountain lion in recovery? I hope he's doped up so he won't move until tomorrow."

Panic fluttered in my chest and I rushed to explain.

"He's on 100 mg. of xylazine and 100 mg. of romifidine every four hours. Tyler is the pet of a family friend. He's been raised by humans since a cub, so he's no danger to you. If something happens to him, I'll never forgive myself." My voice broke and Claire rushed forward.

"Oh, don't worry. I'm sorry. I'll look after him like he was my own pet, I promise."

Claire stroked her hand down my arm and I took a long, shuddering breath. I was holding onto my tears like a starving woman to food. I couldn't fall apart. Not yet.

"I...need to go home, but if you need me, if he struggles to breathe for one moment...you call."

I blew out a breath and wiped at the tears sitting on my lashes. What a fucking long day.

"Of course, I will. No problem at all."

I grabbed my bag, numbness stealing through my rapidly cooling body. I made it out the front door and headed toward her car.

Brandon snagged me as I walked past and pulled me into his body. "I'll drive; jump in."

I couldn't look at him, but allowed him to guide me into his car and drive the few minutes back home. When we arrived, I struggled out the door and started up the sidewalk.

Brandon's strong hands wound around my arms like the roots of a tree, giving me strength when I needed it. He took my keys when my hands shook too much to open the front door, and led me into my bedroom when I stumbled on the carpet.

I tugged at my dirty, sweaty clothes, wanting to be rid of any evidence that today had occurred. When I was down to my underwear, I fell toward the bed, pulling back the covers and climbing in. I rolled over, and hot flesh pressed against my back.

"Thank you for saving my brother's life."

Pain slid through my chest, shattering the cold cloud that had consumed me. "He wouldn't have..." My voice cracked and I stopped talking, raising my hand and pressing it against my mouth in the hope it would stem the sob that was rising.

The truth is, Tyler *could* have died. He nearly had.

"Wouldn't what?" Brandon probed, running his hand up and down my arm in a move that was both reassuring and devastating.

He was being so kind, so thoughtful... like he had been all week.

Oh, God, what have I done?

Sobs rose and escaped my lips. Tears rolled down my cheeks and snot blocked my nose so that I couldn't breathe. I had no strength to fight it anymore, I let it all go. The devastation from last night, the breakup this morning. Then the horrendous ordeal of having to operate on a man I loved.

There was a reason I'd become a veterinarian and didn't go into medicine, and that was because I didn't like cutting *people* open.

"Shh, baby girl. You're okay. I've got you." Brandon held me and didn't try and stop me from crying. His arms were like a tight band around me and the tears kept flowing. I seemed unable to put the brakes on once I'd released them.

"Oh sweetheart, please stop. You're only hurting yourself."

I let the pain descend and consume me. I deserved it.

The tears finally subsided and I wiped them away with fresh tissues Brandon handed me. I let him pull me into his arms. It was nice to be held, though I didn't know why he was bothering.

I'd ended everything between us, and there was no going back now.

"How are you feeling now?"

He seemed to be holding his breath and I shrugged, wiping at the tears that gathered and fell once more. What was wrong with my eyes?

Brandon squeezed me tight and asked again, "Seriously, Laura. You okay?"

I blinked a few times, my eyes sore and scratchy. "I feel numb."

And I did.

There was little else going through my body now. I could barely even feel my arms as I raised them to wipe my cheeks. My tear ducts seemed to be the only things in tune with my pain. The rest of me had shut down. Even my brain was no longer processing anything. I closed my eyes tightly and willed sleep to take me.

"I can't allow that, sweetheart."

Brandon rolled me over and got up on his knees beside me. He pulled my underwear down my legs and I didn't stop him. I opened my legs to welcome him and a part of my depressed brain hoped he'd just fuck me like he did all those other women. I needed the distraction, to be punished for being selfish and stupid.

I hadn't even given the guys a chance to explain.

I'd been judge, jury and executioner. A flaw my mom had often told me off for.

"Damn, you're beautiful."

I sobbed again, covering my wet face with both hands.

Brandon's fingers slid up my thighs and gently traced the flesh between my legs.

"Inside and out, you're gorgeous. I want you to feel how much I care about you. How sorry I am about how badly those girls treated you on Friday. It was all bullshit. Lies. And I'll prove it to you, if you'll just give me the chance."

I nodded my head but didn't really believe him. How could he make this pain go away with sex? The ache was so great I couldn't help the tears that flowed down my cheeks still, but the sobs stopped as he lowered himself down and set his mouth to my clit.

Gentle sensations of pleasure lapped at me while Brandon gently licked me, running his tongue around the sensitive nub of flesh, then licking my closed entrance.

"You're ours, Laura. Our beautiful lover. Never be sorry for what happened this morning."

His wet, warm tongue slipped over my flesh again and something cracked open inside me as Brandon continued to love my body.

I moaned and arched, not caring if it didn't feel the same as it usually did. He was touching me, loving me with his mouth.

His hands tightened on my thighs as he thrust his tongue into me, over and over again. Pleasure filtered down on me like light rain.

Brandon hopped up and prowled over me, his huge frame blocking out the light, and I let my eyes close as he slid into me. I gasped and my eyes flew open, sparkles of energy and love exploding inside me.

"Mine." Brandon growled, the sound making my heart thump against my chest. I placed my hands on his huge arms but left my legs down on the bed.

He began to move, pulling back and seating himself again, the rhythm soothing, slow.

Brandon dropped himself closer and spoke into my ear. "Do you know how much we want you, how we care for you... like we've never cared about anyone before?"

A wounded noise escaped my throat as the words punctured the numbness around me. I lifted my legs and wrapped them around Brandon's hips. He surged harder, pleasure spiraling up through my pelvis. Flames burst out of the dead embers of my emotions and I gasped and bucked my hips up against Brandon.

"We had sex, Laura. Lots of it, in the past. We can't change that. But it is in the past now. Firmly and forever. We were looking for our mate. We were looking for *you*."

He thrust again, deep, and his words hit a chord inside me. "We've found you, Laura, and that changes everything, for both Tyler and me. You are meant to be with us and we will worship you forever. I promise. There is no one else. There never will be again."

Brandon's words sparked a connection somewhere between my cold body and my heart that yearned for him, joining the two threads together.

"Never leave us again, Laura. *Please*! We won't survive without you."

I cried out and clenched tightly around his surging body, sinking my teeth into his shoulder as I battled to hold back the flow of feelings.

He hadn't said it, but I knew he loved me. I could *feel* it coming from him like a wave of sensation. As though his love was a tangible thing within my reach.

"I've always pulled out Laura... always." Brandon groaned. "But I want to cum in you. Do you want that too?"

"Yes!" I dug my nails in harder as my orgasm took control of my body, sweeping me up in one long, intense moment of bliss.

Brandon roared in my ear as his heat filled my belly, pushing me into another full-blown orgasm right on top of the last.

When the shudders finally stopped, I clung to him.

"Thank you," I said, kissing his face, his shoulders, unable to contain the tears of joy.

Somehow, he'd managed to drag me out of despair by reaching into my body and finding my love for him, and gifting me with his in return.

Brandon lifted his head and kissed my lips gently, trembling as he pulled away, then tucked us into a sleeping position.

His lips pressed against my shoulder and I smiled into the semi-darkness. Peace settled over us and I drifted off to sleep, waking later to more lovemaking from Brandon, and a late supper in bed.

Brandon didn't leave me alone for a moment during the night, and I knew that my love for this man was more than complete.

But could I accept them for who they were?

I wanted to, more than anything... but only time would tell if I actually could.

BRANDON

Back at our house, I opened the carved front door and directed the men who carried Tyler on a stretcher, still in mountain lion form. "Bring him in here."

I gestured to Tyler's bedroom, that Laura had set up with equipment to keep him hydrated and out of pain. The men lay Tyler down and cautiously stepped back.

I patted them on the back as they left, chuckling to myself. So many people were afraid of large cats, and rightly so. A wild mountain lion—even an injured one—could rip your arm off.

I waited for the front door to close, signaling that the men had left, then turned to grin down at my brother.

He's home.

I couldn't see Tyler's shoulder through the bandages, but it wouldn't be long now. He'd heal quickly, now that he was in his own environment.

Laura entered the room and ran a hand down Tyler's front paw. "His breathing and blood pressure are normal. I don't think it'll be long before he wakes."

"Great."

I watched with relief as my brother's lion body transformed back into his human one. Golden fur disappeared as skin reappeared. His limbs elongated and thickened as his head and torso reshaped and grew.

A groan sounded—more frustration than pain. "Thank God for that." Tyler's voice was weak but laced with humor. "I've been wanting to shift for hours but they were watching me too closely."

Tyler turned onto his back and grimaced, running his hand over his injured shoulder. Laura threw herself down onto the bed with a cry and wrapped her arms around him.

"What's happening? Laura? Oh, sweetheart, are you okay?"

Laura was sobbing her heart out and burying her head in Tyler's neck like she was trying to become part of him.

Tyler looked up at me with a panicked expression and a hand signal for help.

I grinned and walked over, staring down at the two of them with a heart close to bursting. Laura and I had started the process of mending our rift, though we still had a lot to discuss.

Dealing with Simone's false accusations for one thing.

But in the face of death, that could be put aside for the moment. Now Laura had to reunite with Tyler—in human form and not possibly dying on her operating table. I should probably leave them alone... do the honorable and selfless thing.

Fuck that.

I wasn't missing out on a chance to be inside Laura's hot body again. "Good to see you, brother."

Tyler looked at me, confusion evident in his eyes as he stroked Laura's long brown hair. "You too, bro. Sorry about yesterday."

I nodded and placed my hand on Tyler's ankle for a moment. We'd both said some stupid things at our parent's place in the heat of the moment, but nothing that couldn't be forgotten just as quickly. "Yeah, me too."

Tyler shifted his attention back to Laura, forcing her head up by grabbing her chin. "Hey, hey, what's with all the tears? The last thing I remember—other than the agony of being shot—is you breaking up with us because we'd slept around too much before we met you."

Laura sobbed once more and shook her head, snuffling like a seal. "I was jealous."

Tyler's eyes widened in surprise. "Jealous of what? Those stupid whores? They're in the past, beautiful. Now we've met you, no one else matters."

Laura drew back a little, but didn't quite let go of Tyler. "They knew so many intimate details about you and what you do in bed and I..."

"You what?"

She shrugged. "I didn't feel special anymore."

Tyler laughed. "Oh, sweetheart, how can you say that?"

"Because they were so descriptive and vile! It made me want to vomit. I could just see you... licking them, making love to them, the way they described."

"Nope. Hold on right there. We never made love to any of them. Not one. The only one I've ever *made love* with, is you. As far as my skill set is concerned, honey, all of it was practice for you. I wanted to be the best lover I could possibly be, so that when my mate came along, she'd never leave me."

Laura didn't say anything.

Tyler looked at me for help.

I cleared my throat. "It's true, Laura. It's not easy being male and a good lover. Our bodies are designed to get in, deposit the seed, and get out. Lions mate for all of ten seconds."

That got a laugh out of her, but I continued, because she had to know the truth. "Sweetheart, there is no comparison between the way I make love to you and the way I used to fuck other women. They were sport. Exercise. A way to kill time before meeting you. Nothing more."

She met my gaze and assessed me as she always did, with those searching green eyes of hers. "You mean it?" She shifted her gaze to Tyler. "You both do?"

"Of course, we do!" I spoke more vehemently than I meant to, but she had to know the truth. There was no one else for us. Not anymore.

"And you still want me? Even though I can tell you that this *is* going to come up again. I'm gonna have issues and insecurities, and if I see one of those women in public I'm probably going to cry again. I just can't imagine you ever wanting me after I saw what you normally go for."

Tyler growled and pulled her close. "Of course, we want you. And only you, beautiful. You're a real woman. They were plastic Barbie dolls that we could walk away from at the end of the day. You're the woman we want to birth our babies and stay with forever. We've been waiting our whole lives for you."

A smile spread across her face.

Laura grinned at Tyler like the sun had finally come out to play. Like the clouds had cleared in Laura's deep, dark world.

She rolled away for a tissue and cleaned up her face before sliding back into place next to Tyler. "So, you really do want me, huh? To be your... mate?" She smiled up at Tyler and I chuckled.

Tyler kissed her lips gently. "More than I've ever wanted anyone, beautiful girl."

Laura let out the sweetest giggle and I grinned. I loved hearing her so happy.

Then she did the last thing I expected. She slithered down Tyler's belly and took his cock into her mouth, moaning like a woman who'd just discovered chocolate for the first time.

Hell, yeah.

Tyler gripped her head and gasped as she worked his flesh,

similar feelings of pleasure engulfing my cock while I stripped off my clinging clothes. My skin burned like it did when I was about to shift, but I wasn't going to. Instead, I was aching to bond with Laura, the ménage mating that my family had predicted I needed calling to me like never before.

I stood and watched as Laura pleasured my brother, my own cock rising and tingling as I studied her beautiful mouth, imagining her lips on me.

Tyler and I were linked, more than I ever thought possible.

If...no, *when,* we mated Laura, I knew that pleasure unlike anything I had ever known awaited me.

"Up on your knees, babe." I tapped Laura's ass and she suddenly pulled back off the bed with a wild look in her green eyes.

She ripped off her clothes in a flurry of jeans and cotton, then resumed sucking Tyler's cock while on all fours for me, bobbing her head in a hypnotic rhythm.

I stared at my beloved woman and groaned as the erotic picture she made sent heat blazing through my blood. My cock throbbed, yet I waited to penetrate her, bending forward and setting my tongue against her already-glistening slit.

Honeysuckle burst across my tongue as Laura squealed and pushed back against me.

I moved my mouth from ass to clit, tasting her swollen, hot flesh, and moaning as my cock swelled and hardened.

God, how I lust after this woman.

Tyler's strangled voice said, "Beautiful, you need to ride me."

Her cunt disappeared from beneath my tongue and Laura got up and straddled Tyler before I could blink.

I watched as Laura gripped Tyler's dick in her fist and impaled herself, the sight of her cunt swallowing up Tyler's cock almost enough to make me blow on the spot.

I took a steadying breath and marveled at the sensations pulsing through me. Not as strong as if Laura were on me, but an echo of that tight squeeze wrapped around my shaft.

Laura began really moving on Tyler, their flesh slapping together as Tyler thrust up and she pounded down.

"Oh, fuck, I'm gonna..."

Laura cried out as Tyler came inside her, throwing her head back and gasping as my brother squeezed her hips hard.

My turn.

With my heart pounding an erratic tattoo against my ribs, I reached over and grabbed Laura around her waist, then flipped her over.

She landed on her back and I was on top of her in an instant, kissing her perfect pink lips and pressing my cock into her pussy.

"Please! Yes!" Laura cried out, grabbing my ass and pulling me into her in a move that smacked of desperation.

I didn't make her wait. I slammed into her, the front of my thighs connecting with hers, over and over again.

She screamed and came, clamping down on my cock and milking me hard as I continued to fuck her through her climax.

Over and over, I thrust into her tight, welcoming body, closing my eyes and opening my mind up to the rainbow of new sensations available to me.

Fucking hell!

Laura touched my very soul when we were joined like this.

Love rained down upon me like sunshine in the middle of summer, and I never wanted to step away from the light again. Her breath was hot against my neck as she licked and kissed whatever skin she could get to, her hips rising in time with my thrusts.

She began to make keening noises, her cunt quivering around me. My balls tightened and my cock began screaming at me with sensation. I was so gone.

"Brandon!"

My eyes snapped open to see her green gaze staring at me, wonder and love glowing like embers in a dying fire. I began to come and thrust deeply inside my mate, planting the seeds of my need for her.

Laura shuddered over me and heat rolled down my back as my orgasm sucked me under the wave.

Laura's chest rose and fell at a rapid rate, her hands gripping my hair and holding me to her. "Oh, thank you, thank you." She let out a strange sob and clung to me.

Something inside my chest cracked open like the final stage of a butterfly emerging from its cocoon, transforming me into something incredible.

Something *better*.

I'd do everything in my power to make sure this woman was always loved, wanted and appreciated. I would devote my life to that goal.

"You okay?" I asked as I kissed her ear and rolled to the side so that she was once again in between Tyler and me.

"Okay? Much better than okay." She laughed and stroked her hands down my chest, then turned her head and reached over to touch Tyler as well.

"Tyler, you feeling all right, or should I get some more painkillers?"

Soft snoring reached our ears and I looked over to see my twin brother had passed out.

I chuckled and pulled Laura against my chest. "Looks like he needs more rest. You wore him out."

Laura giggled and snuggled closer. I began to close my eyes when she gasped and lifted her head, an incredibly beautiful smile lighting up her face. "Wanna have a quick shower? I've been dying to try out that double-nozzled shower head."

I kissed her nose and nodded. *Why not?* "Let's go."

Laura bounced up and off the bed, laughing as she ran to the bathroom and turned on the water. I sat up slowly and slid off the bed with a sense of purpose.

I strode toward the bathroom with my resolve firmly in place. My woman would never regret loving me.

BRANDON

19

My phone vibrated in my pocket and I pulled it out. A name came up on the caller ID that I did not want to see, and I found himself glaring at it.

Fuck!

I hadn't gotten around to blocking her yet. "Sorry babe, it's Simone."

I waved the phone at Laura, aware that she may blow a gasket any moment, but I wasn't lying about anything—not even the little things.

Laura frowned. "Have you approached her about her lies yet?"

An idea formed that brought a grin to my face. "No, I haven't. Might be time to do that, don't you think?"

I placed the phone on the table, hit the green button and the speaker button in two pushes. "Simone, you lying little bitch."

Simone's gasp, then giggle, hit me in the gut and I clenched my teeth against the need to growl out a warning.

Laura gagged on the other side of the kitchen counter.

I winked at my woman and watched a small smile spread across her face. This was risky. Simone could be one nasty piece of work, but it would be worth the risk to reassure Laura that I hadn't been cheating on her.

"What's wrong, Brandon? Have you missed me?"

Her voice was sickly sweet and I couldn't repress the shudder that rose. God, she was cold. "Not one tiny little bit, sweetheart. But I would like to know why you told Laura that we were together last Friday night."

There was silence on the other end of the line and I waited.

My ex-fuck-buddy might hang up instead of attempting to justify her bullshit.

"Come on, Simone. You always have a reason."

"You deserve better than someone like that, Brandon. She was fat *and* ugly and human too! What a terrible combination for you. Plus, you know she'll *never* be able to satisfy you the way I can." She let out a purr that made me shudder once again.

I'd had a threesome or two with Simone, hoping that if I added in another woman there would be a little warmth or affection that would make the sex more palatable. But no, there had just been more taking by her.

"I don't like you lying about me, Simone." I forced some warmth into my tone, hoping to charm the truth out of her. "It's not polite of you."

She laughed, the sound a little strained now. "I wasn't really lying, Brandon. I saw you running toward the mountain and I shifted to chase you. I know how much you love mating in the moonlight."

I clenched my teeth and lifted my gaze, mouthing *sorry* to Laura.

She fluttered her hands and smiled at me.

I was wavering now. Push forward and get the truth and risk hurting Laura some more, or not?

I leaned my forearms against the cold marble and focused on the phone.

"Yeah, but you didn't find me. I ran to the cave and back and didn't see anyone."

And that was the truth!

She huffed a little. "Yeah, I know. I couldn't catch you and cut my paw on a rock near the pond, so I went home."

I grinned in victory.

I stood up straighter and looked at Laura. She smiled brightly and love filled me up.

"Thanks for straightening that out, Simone. I couldn't have Laura thinking I'd lie to her."

"What? You can't be with her, Brandon. She's not even a shifter!"

I picked up the phone and spoke into the speaker. "Laura is the most beautiful, amazing woman I've ever met, and I wanted you to be the first to know. Let the rest of the women know that Tyler and I are permanently off the market, and any further attempts at destroying our relationship will be met with retribution."

A loud, hissing sound came through the phone as Simone began to boil like a kettle on a burner.

Our pride had very few laws, but my parents were wealthy, respected, and powerful. If necessary, I'd pull every string I had to keep Laura safe and happy.

"You fucking bastard."

I chuckled. "Nope, I know who my parents are, Simone... unlike you. And as for the fucking bit...yeah, I think I'll get back to that."

I hit the End button before she could spew any more poison. I'd had enough of those sorts of females for a lifetime.

Laura slid off her seat and rounded the counter, coming up to me and running her hands up and around my neck. "So, you don't want to keep your options open anymore, huh? No more never-ending smorgasbord of women?"

Her eyes were bright and her tone was cheeky, yet I needed to put this subject to bed once and for all. "I want you, my beautiful girl. No one comes within a mile of your beauty, your sensuality, or your amazing heart."

Laura continued to stare at me as though she expected more.

I faltered.

I loved her and I needed to tell her, but something held the words back.

"Thank you, Brandon. I really appreciate you doing that for me."

She went up on her toes and kissed me, drawing me into her

taste.

When she moved toward the bedroom, I went willingly, and happily kept her there all afternoon.

LAURA

I sat on the bed the following day with my feet tucked up under me.

I'd decided to take a week's leave and give myself time to look after Tyler, and get past the weekend's events.

I stared at my men, because that's what they were, whether they loved me or not. I certainly loved them, or how else could I get over everything so quickly? And I knew one other thing—my heart would never allow another in.

"What's up?" I cocked my head and watched them prowl around the large room in their human form.

I'd love to see them both in lion form at the same time because, as men, they were magnificent to watch—so lithe and graceful, yet powerful and strong. Their muscles flexed beneath their cotton shirts and they were making growly noises that made me wiggle on the bed.

Whenever their mountain lion sides came out, I got a lovemaking session to break the record books. They finally come to a stop, shoulder to shoulder, and stared at me.

"We want you to mate with us," they said in unison.

It would have been funny if it didn't make me want to cry.

Mating with someone was the same as marriage in the shifter world, I was pretty sure.

I wasn't sure I could do that. Not yet. I wasn't ready.

"Ah…" I looked down at my hands, examining the lines of my palms and my too-short fingernails. I'd always wanted pretty, painted fingernails. They looked so elegant when done right. But I couldn't, not with work.

"Laura?" Tyler's gentle voice encouraged me back into reality. I forced myself to raise my head and sighed as longing for my men passed over me.

"I'm sorry, but I can't."

Brandon's jaw hardened and tightened, his blue eyes glittering with rage. "Is this still about those stupid skanks?"

I snapped my gaze to the Viking, clenching my jaw as fire spread over my face. Why didn't they understand how big a deal that was for me?

"It's not just that, but yeah, I'm still worried about that. I know it's not fair to blame you for your past. You made your choices and that's your right."

"It's not like you were a virgin either when we met you, Laura," Brandon fired back.

Ouch. Well-aimed shot.

My chest ached and I slumped. I considered myself a rational woman, and refusing to see beyond their past decisions wasn't fair.

"I don't think three lovers over ten years puts me in the same category as you two." I dropped my gaze again, exhaustion swimming through my muscles. "Can't we discuss this later?"

A growl sounded and I glanced up to see Brandon pacing like a caged animal. "No, we need to deal with this issue once and for all. One woman or a hundred, it's all in the past. It's you that we want now."

"Sure, but for how long? Until another woman passes by and you want her? How can you tell me that you just want me after all the variety you've had? And I've seen them, Brandon. They're all blonde and skinny. I don't even know how you can touch me after them..." I trailed off and bit my lip as the tears rose again. "I'll stay with you as long as you'll have me, but I just can't..."

How could I explain it better?

Mating would be like a human marriage, and where would I be when they moved on to someone else? I'd be broken, discarded. I wouldn't survive that.

Brandon walked forward and fell to his knees in front of me, taking my hands in his. His eyes were beseeching as he spoke. "You have no idea how much better it is with you."

I sniffed and focused on his words. My brain was utterly exhausted from going over this too many times. "What's better?"

He grinned at me, that lopsided, ultimately charming smile that I adored. "Everything! Including the fucking."

"Oh, you…" Fire flared in my belly and I tried to pull my hands back, but he held tight to them.

"Laura. I've never been with a woman who makes me feel so free, so relaxed. Everything with you is easy and natural, and you blow my fucking mind with how much you give."

"Give?" I repeated and stopped struggling, not sure I understood.

"You touch me and give me pleasure. You aren't focused on yourself."

What was he talking about?

"Of course, I'm not. Nothing feels better to me than hearing you losing control, the way your face looks when I suck you…or touch you."

"You take me places no one has. I love you for that. And a thousand other reasons."

I couldn't have heard right. Brandon had avoided talk of love like the plague the last few days, despite everything we'd gone through.

"Did you say you love me?"

Brandon swallowed, his large Adam's apple bobbing up and down. "Ah, yeah."

My heart burst open, with happiness surging in my chest. "I really don't think…"

"Please Laura, you have to listen to us."

I turned toward Tyler, who sat on the bed next to me, cupping my face with his smooth, gentle hands.

"You're everything I've ever wanted in a woman. You are intelligent, smart, and beautiful. And best of all, you have the warmest, most giving heart. The way you love Brandon and me—it's the best thing ever."

Tears prickled my eyes and I tried to blink them back, but staring at the adoring faces of my men made it impossible.

"I...I..." I had at least ten reasons ready as to why we shouldn't be together, but as both of my magnificent lion shifters stood up and began stripping off their clothes, I couldn't think of a single one.

"We're going to make love to you, and prove to you how much we love you," Tyler, my amazing wordsmith, said.

I glanced over at Brandon and watched him strip the last of his clothes, his cock already thickening.

"Hmmm." I hummed as I slid to the floor and took his cock into my mouth.

Brandon grabbed me by the hair and pulled my head back. It stung a little but I looked up, anxious to know what he wanted.

"Why do you do that?" he asked. "Tell me."

He wanted the words. At first, I wasn't sure I could say them. Then they just blurted out. "Because...I like feeling it getting thicker and harder in my mouth."

Brandon nodded, his lips opening as he took a deep breath and guided me back to his cock. I took the hot, steel-like flesh in my mouth and sucked hard, exulting in the groans that slipped from Brandon's mouth. "Strip and kneel on the bed, beautiful."

I jumped up and began pulling at my clothes. I was so hot and ready for them. I got down to my underpants and waited for Tyler since he always liked undressing me.

"No. You take them off," Brandon said, his tone deeper than it had ever been, his eyes pinned on my face.

I slid my panties down my thighs, hating the insecurity swamping me. It was the middle of the day, full daylight. They'd be able to see the cellulite, the white stretch marks on my hips and breasts, my *fat*.

Fuck it.

I slipped my bra off too, and stood perfectly still, willing the tears away and kept my chin high.

"Do you know what I see?" Brandon drawled.

I shook my head and tears spilled down my cheeks. Were they really going to list all my faults?

"The sexiest woman I've ever met."

I frowned and finally allowed myself to cover my breasts with my arms, lifting them up so they didn't sag. "Don't lie, Brandon."

Brandon took a step forward and grabbed one of my hands, drawing it down to his rock-hard cock. "You feel this? This doesn't lie. I need to fuck you. Get on your knees on the bed, head down."

I didn't stop to think, just whirled around and spread my knees and dropped my head, presenting to Brandon exactly the way he asked.

"Now this is my favorite position," he said with a sigh.

I couldn't stop the words from tripping off my tongue. "Of course, it is. You can't see my face."

Slap.

Brandon's hand cracked across my ass and pain rippled over my rump. "Ow!" I complained, though he soothed the hurt with his palm.

"See this curve..." He slid the pads of his fingertips over my buttocks, one butt cheek at a time. "It is *fucking* hot." He purred like a contented cat and slowly traced the flesh he was admiring, leaving a trail of sensitive skin that begged for more attention.

I shivered and pushed my hips back as heat pooled between my thighs.

"And this... this is where I go to heaven." Brandon slid his fingers over my aching cleft and down to my clit, circling the bud and flicking it with his talented digits.

Tingles of pleasure spread through my belly, igniting my need for this man. "Brandon...please." I pressed back, opening myself completely for him to see my body.

"And *that* is why I love this position. You show me how much you want me."

"Of course, I want you. I need you." I panted for breath, feeling the buildup inside my belly as Brandon gently traced the curves of my ass and teased my sensitive lips.

"You want my cock in your cunt, Laura?" Brandon asked, his deliberately crude words making me squirm and press my face into the cotton blanket. Why did such a question make me hot for him?

"Laura?" Brandon repeated, the smooth head of his cock kissing my wet entrance.

"Yes." I pressed back and he moved away. The loss of his flesh hurt, and I moved back to my original position.

Brandon fell to the mattress beside me and pulled me over to straddle his waist.

He stared up at me, his face open and honest. "I love you. Tyler loves you. Bonding for us is more important than marriage. It is irreversible and will bind our souls together forever."

I bit my lip and trembled, despite the heat of the room. If that were true, then I really would have everything I'd ever wanted.

Unconditional love and trust. Forever more.

"You'd never cheat on me?" I asked.

Brandon laughed. "We couldn't do it. Our mating to you would be absolute and complete. Forever."

He waited and finally asked again. "Will you accept us?"

Tyler crawled onto the bed and kneeled next to me, his eyes imploring me to choose. But there was no choice, and that was the real reason I was scared.

"Of course, I will. I love you both so much. I can't live without you." My heart on my sleeve, I held my breath and waited for them to respond.

"Oh, thank God for that!" Brandon squeezed his eyes shut and Tyler swooped in, kissing me breathless.

"We both need to be inside you, beautiful. Do you think you can do that?" Tyler held my gaze and it took a moment to realize what he meant.

"I haven't...ah, yes. All right."

I hadn't taken in a man like that before. But I'd do anything to keep my men happy.

Tyler pressed one more kiss to my lips. "I'll go find some lube. Be back in a moment."

I tried not to think about that, and luckily, I didn't need to. Brandon was kneading my breasts, drawing them down to suckle. I gasped and wriggled on him, streams of pleasure arrowing through my belly and into my pussy.

I needed them so much.

Brandon was rotating his hips and moaning as he sucked on my nipples.

I pulled away and began rubbing my aching pussy along the length of his hard cock. "I want you inside me."

Brandon let my breast slip from his lips and grinned up at me. "Then take me."

I reached for Brandon's cock, wrapped my hand around the thick shaft and lifted it to line up with my body.

I pressed back and down, taking Brandon into me with a sigh of acceptance and peace. He filled me up and completed me, yet I could feel the need for Tyler, too.

I looked over my shoulder and saw my other mate stroking his cock with oil and staring at me. "I love you, Tyler."

He smiled back at me, his eyes bright and glowing almost yellow. "I love you, beautiful girl."

Tyler pressed on my back. "Lean down and kiss Brandon."

I pressed my breasts to Brandon's chest, kissing my big mountain lion and whispering. "I love you, Brandon."

He lifted my chin with his fingers and kissed my lips. "I love you, Laura."

Tyler's fingers pressed against my ass and I shivered. It was a strange sensation, and a little intimidating, too.

Brandon began to move, thrusting up into my pussy in shallow, slow movements. "Relax, gorgeous."

I closed my eyes and focused on the sensations Brandon was

creating. My womb was pulsing, my body craving my men.

Tyler's lubricated finger teased my asshole and I pressed back. He interpreted my movement correctly and slid a finger inside me.

It wasn't too bad, though it burned. I moved my hips a little faster and Tyler slid a second finger in and began stretching me.

That stole my breath as the burning increased, but didn't seem to dampen my body's needs. In fact, my desire increased.

I was *aching* in my back passage, wanting a deeper contact. Feeling... *empty.*

I opened my eyes and Brandon's eyes glowed yellow, his lion merging with his human body for the mating.

Tyler's fingers disappeared and I cried out at the loss. "No! Put them back."

I turned my head around and watched as Tyler mounted me, cock in hand. "I will, sweetheart. You relax. Feel us inside of you."

I forced my body to go limp and cried out as Tyler pressed forward, a small twinge and burn, then an incredible fullness. "Oh, fuck, that feels amazing."

Brandon panted beneath me, his cock twitching inside me, but he wasn't moving any longer.

I was boiling with pressure. "Move. Please."

I bumped my hips back and forth against them and they surged as one. "Oh, fuck!" Brandon groaned.

Tyler pulled back, then thrust forward, Brandon doing the opposite and hissing between his teeth.

They established a counter-rhythm that had me screaming out.

My body was in raptures as my men stoked the fire within me higher and higher. My belly began to tighten and my orgasm swelled. "Oh my..."

I broke apart, my body convulsing around my men as I screamed and begged them to join me.

Brandon cried out first, thrusting up and spilling his seed inside me while he sank his teeth into my shoulder. Pain made me cry out, yet it disappeared as fast as it had come.

Two more thrusts and Tyler's hoarse cries rang through the air and heat flooded my body again, his teeth biting into my opposite shoulder.

I collapsed onto Brandon's chest, panting hard and unable to open my eyes. Every cell of my body, every corner of my soul, was sated.

I'd never been so at peace, so genuinely blissful. I'd found everything I would ever need in this bedroom.

Tyler pulled out and collapsed next to us, pulling me over so that Brandon rolled and they sandwiched me between them.

I looked down at my body, expecting to see something different; a change. My whole world had tilted on its axis. Surely there would be a sign?

"I won't turn into a mountain lion now, will I?"

Brandon chuckled. "No, baby. Shifters are born, not made."

I sighed and settled against them, letting contentment wash over me like a cleansing rain.

"Though... you will carry our marks forever."

Brandon traced the place over my shoulder where he'd bitten me and I forced my eyes open to see a set of feline bite marks the size of a human's jaw.

Whoa.

I whipped my head around to the other side and laughed as I saw the twin marking. They were positioned so that no one would ever see them if I wore a tank, not that it mattered. I'd entered a new world now. The old rules didn't matter. "Good. Now everyone will know I'm yours."

Brandon grunted and kissed her hair. "Damn straight."

"You complete us, Laura. You're our center... our whole world." Tyler kissed my neck and I sighed.

They were my everything.

I knew in my heart of hearts that as long as I trusted them and loved them as they did me there was no hurdle we couldn't fly over together.

LAURA

EPILOGUE

Three Months Later

"Laura, Brandon, and Tyler, you are now bonded for life."

A roar went up around us and I lifted my face toward my men.

I was so happy I could barely contain the scream of excitement that threatened to let loose. Brandon kissed me first, his mouth possessive and strong, his tongue slipping in to taste me.

When he stepped away, Tyler slid into his place, cupping my face and kissing me with such sweetness and love that tears slipped down my cheeks.

My perfect pair. Everything I'd ever wanted, and so much more.

"I love you," Tyler whispered against my lips as he pulled back. I looked into his brown eyes, blinking away the happy tears that had gathered once again.

"And I love you."

I extended my hand and Brandon gripped it. "I love you," I said to my big lion, who grinned and winked.

Classic Brandon.

But his eyes spoke volumes. *I love you*, he mouthed, and I squeezed his hand.

I know.

Tyler turned me toward the group of people who had gathered on Tyler and Brandon's parents' property to witness our mating.

I had legally married Tyler during the week in a small ceremony surrounded by our family and friends, but this was the more important of the two ceremonies. "Let's celebrate."

I was pulled forward into a maelstrom of people.

Hugs, kisses, and congratulations flowed around me as I was whirled from one set of strong arms to another.

By the time they'd all finished taking a piece of me, I could barely stand up. I collapsed onto a garden seat, gasping for breath in my tight wedding dress. "Laura, you look absolutely beautiful."

Scott and Jack stood before me, looking powerful and handsome in their black suits. "Wow, you two look amazing."

They inclined their heads, but seemed distracted, their eyes continually straying to an area near the food tables.

I turned and looked in the same direction but couldn't see anything of note. "What are you two staring at so intently?"

I put out a hand and Jack lifted me to my feet. "Oh, that's better." My bodice was boned, giving my waist a beautiful indent, but it wasn't the easiest thing to maneuver around in.

"Laura, who is that woman in the gray silk dress?" Scott asked.

That's interesting.

That was a lot of detail for a man to notice, and what was with the tone of his voice?

I turned around again and scanned the area, happiness filling my chest when I realized who they were talking about.

"Oh, she came!" I clapped my hands and took a step in that direction.

Scott's hand came around my arm as quickly as a rattlesnake and stopped me in my tracks. "Is she a friend of yours, Laura?"

Scott's voice was even deeper now, raspy even.

I stared at him, then at Jack, then back to the woman in question.

Uh-oh.

"Yes...she's my cousin from up north. I invited her to my wedding with Tyler but she couldn't come as it was held during the week. So, I told her about today but said it started at three rather than two, so she'd miss the ceremony itself. Although..." I tapped my foot and pulled my arm out of Scott's grip.

"I won't be upset if she knows about Tyler *and* Brandon. My family will work it out eventually."

My sister had been great, supporting me as much as she could given she was now settled into university.

But she was also envious of my relationship, and even though she'd been a bridesmaid for me today, she was currently standing about ten feet away, scanning the area for more sets of twins for herself.

"Can you introduce us to her?" Jack asked, his face showing a weird type of strain that I hadn't seen before on this man.

But I *had* seen it on Tyler and Brandon.

"Sure." I walked through the throng of people and made my way to Ashleigh's side. If I was right, then my gorgeous cousin's life was about to change forever.

"You came!" I threw myself on her and hugged her tightly. Ashleigh, a few years older than me, had doted on me when I was a child.

Ashleigh laughed and hugged me back, our heights and sizes in almost exact proportion. I pulled back and stared at her. I hadn't seen Ashleigh in five years and she didn't look as well as I expected. "You look like shit, Ash. I don't want to be rude, but are you okay, hon?"

Ashleigh smiled, though sadness was evident in her beautiful blue eyes. The radiance I remembered about my older cousin was gone, the glow of her skin tinged with gray. What had happened?

"Thanks, sweetie, I know. Whereas you look freaking fantastic."

I did a twirl and stuck my hip out at an angle, playing the game. "Why, thank you, darling. The love of a good man, and all that."

Ash quirked an eyebrow at me. "Or men, perhaps?"

Heat flooded my cheeks and my stomach dropped. I searched my cousin's face for signs of discrimination or disgust, but there was none. "Yeah...well..."

Ashleigh chuckled, and reached over to squeeze my hand. "As long as you're happy, honey."

I nodded and the heat of a man pressed up behind me.

Scott was standing there, almost dancing on the spot in his impatience. I'd forgotten he and Jack were even there.

"Oh, Ash, let me introduce you to Brandon and Tyler's cousins. It's common in their family for men to be born into fraternal twin sets. This is Scott and Jack. Guys, this is my cousin, Ashleigh."

Scott and Jack jumped up beside me like Army basic training graduates, their backs ramrod straight.

Ashleigh's face turned cold, her mouth pulling down on both sides. "Nice to meet you, gentlemen."

The men stuck out their hands and I knew what they were thinking. They wanted to touch her so they could gauge her response.

Oh my God, is Ashleigh their chosen mate?

Ash looked at the men's hands as though they were rats crawling through her room, but neither Jack nor Scott dropped their hands.

Finally, Ashleigh sighed and reached up to shake Scott's hand.

Watching it happen rather than experiencing it was one of the weirdest things I'd ever seen.

Ashleigh gasped and her face filled with blood, her knees obviously weakening as she sank closer to the ground.

Jack jumped forward to catch her and they both groaned as their bodies came into contact.

Ashleigh's eyes widened and she dropped Scott's hand to cling to Jack, who was still holding her.

Jack managed to continue to stand, though he looked shaky, too.

All three stared at each other with varying degrees of shock and lust. Ashleigh finally straightened, anger clouding her face as she pushed herself out of Jack's arms. Then she staggered toward me.

I grabbed my cousin, holding her arms and supporting some of her weight. I knew how confusing such a moment could be.

"What the fuck was that?" Ash spat the words at them, her tone harsh enough to make the men around us growl a little.

Scott and Jack stared at me, their eyes burning with something painful. So much hurt, love and need.

It was too intense for me to handle as an observer, and I had to look away.

I focused on my trembling cousin. "Ash, how long are you here for?"

Ashleigh straightened up and looked into my eyes. She wasn't the same person I'd known all those years ago. Something about her felt off.

"A week or so. I took some leave."

That was fantastic. Maybe Scott and Jack could put some sunshine back into Ash's world. "Brilliant. We're only going away for the weekend, but we have honeymoon plans for later in the summer. Will you stay with us through next week?"

Ash looked back at Scott and Jack for a moment, frowning, then back at me, nodding slowly. "Yeah, sure. I'd love to catch up."

Jack cleared his throat and held out his hand to Ash once again. "Would you like a tour of the property?"

Ash glared at him, her blue eyes firing ice chips. "No fucking way, and keep your hands to yourself."

She turned tail and headed off, her chin stuck high in the air as she stomped her way up the steps and back into the house.

A giggle bubbled up and escaped my throat.

I turned to face the shocked men. "You two are going to have your hands full with Ash if she's yours."

"She is ours," the men said in unison, their voices deep and growly.

Brandon and Tyler's hands slid around my waist and I smiled as I was engulfed in the heat of their bodies.

"Hey Scott, Jack." Brandon's deep voice made me sigh and lean toward him.

The men nodded mechanically, their eyes straying to the house again.

"Congratulations to you all. Ah...we..." They began to edge away and I laughed, waving my hands at them.

"Go, go. I've asked her to stay at my place, so I'll get the boys to send you my address. You have the weekend with her, then I'll have her from Monday."

Their gorgeous faces broke into identical grins and they headed off without a backward glance. I sighed and watched them hurry away. Was that what my men had gone through?

"What's up with them?" Brandon asked, while Tyler stroked my hand in rhythmic possession.

I looked up into Brandon's blue eyes. "My cousin Ashleigh is their mate."

Brandon's eyes widened. "You're shitting me?"

I laughed out loud. "Nope. Looks like there's something about my family that mingles well with you boys."

Tyler slid his hand over my abdomen and rubbed gently. "Will we be seeing how our blood mingles soon?"

I inhaled sharply. I hadn't thought they'd noticed.

I nodded. I'd gone off the pill as soon as we'd ironed things out a few months ago and my period was now a week late. I'd taken a home test that morning. "I haven't been to a doctor yet, but yes... I'm pretty sure we're going to have a baby."

Tyler's face lit up in a spectacular grin and Brandon picked me up in his arms, twirling me and whooping loudly.

"Hey, hey, hey, put me down." My head was spinning.

Brandon placed me down and kissed me until my head was clouded with need. I sank into his embrace and Tyler's lips pressed against my neck.

My belly quivered as I lifted my arm, sliding one hand into Brandon's hair and the other into Tyler's, holding my men to me, where they were forever meant to be.

THE END

~

I hope you enjoyed 'Prowling their Mate'. The next book,
'Stalking their Mate,' – Ashleigh, Jack and Scott's story, is out now!

You can download: https://books2read.com/stalkingtheirmate
Or read on for a sneak peek:

~

JACK

1

I grinned and whooped loudly, happiness for the couple in front of me flowing through my blood like rich wine, giving me a sense of warmth and satisfaction.

Though, was it still a couple if there were three of them? Probably not.

I hadn't worried about what to call them before now. We didn't have many ménage relationships in our family yet.

Laura, the bride, lifted her face toward her men.

Brandon, my big cousin, kissed her first. Then Tyler, his brother, turned their woman toward him, cupping Laura's face and kissing her also.

A quiver of pain pierced the happiness within my chest, like a needle sliding through a balloon, deflating it. Such a small thing to witness, but oh-so-powerful. The image before me was like a dream. What my brother and I should have.

We were a perfect pair too, just like Tyler and Brandon. But we were a decade or two older. We should have already found our fated woman and mated her long before now.

But we'd both chosen a different path.

In retrospect, we'd chosen the wrong path.

Watching Brandon, Tyler and Laura together made me ache with yearning for what might have been. Iswallowed hard, trying to dislodge the deep-seated feeling.

I copped an elbow in my side from Scott and physical pain spread through my ribs.

Ouch!

"Don't you dare go all maudlin on me today."

I scowled, leaning forward, and hit my brother with a swing of my shoulder. "Why the hell would I do that?"

Scott chuckled and lay his arm across the back of my plastic garden chair. "Because I know you still think she's out there. Some perfect woman made just for us." Scott huffed out a laugh, but there was no humor there. "But you know that won't happen now. We're pushing fifty, Jack. We're done."

I turned and glared at my brother. Scott needed to get over all the crap his wife had put him through and move forward. "You might be done, but I'm not."

Age is a number. Nothing more.

I looked back toward the newly bonded family, taking quick breaths through my nose to calm down. My heart pounded heavier now, mostly with anger, and I shouldn't feel that way at a bonding ceremony.

After the ceremony we mingled for an hour and I enjoyed the light-hearted banter and general good feelings being with my family gave me.

When we finally stopped to get another drink, I scanned the area and watched Laura bounce from one relative to another.

I shook my head with a chuckle.

Poor woman didn't know what she was in for. My gaze drifted around the crowd until it fell upon a beautiful woman standing by the refreshment table.

I blinked as lust punched me in the gut.

"Who is that..."

My gaze devoured the woman. She had shoulder length reddish-brown hair and a sad, beautiful face. Her body was curved in all the right places, yet her silvery-gray slip dress hid most of her abundant flesh from sight.

"Who are you staring at?" Scott turned to stand next to me, shoulder to shoulder, peering in the same direction. "Are you... The woman with..."

He let out a small groan and stumbled a little until he grabbed hold of the back of a chair, still facing the woman.

Thank you, God! We've found her.

"Quick, we need to get to her." I slapped my brother on the knee and Scott growled at me.

"Calm down, Jack. We can't just rush over there. I don't think she has any shifter in her, so she must be from Laura's side."

I nodded, excitement building in me like a running faucet in a bathtub, filling me up to overflowing. I couldn't wait for the moment it happened.

"Okay, so we should talk to Laura first. Ask for an introduction."

I grinned at my brother and pulled Scott to a stand again. A strange feeling flowed between us. A sizzling connection and a joined purpose. I hadn't felt that with Scott since we were teenagers. Before we'd met our wives and been torn apart.

Scott led the way through the thick crowd, and I followed. My breath caught in my throat. I couldn't stop my gaze from darting over to the woman with the auburn hair and I copped another punch to the gut.

God, it was a good feeling after so long.

Alive, I suddenly realized. I felt alive, where I'd felt before like I was merely existing.

We found the lovely bride collapsed on a garden chair, panting with the stress of being thrown from one set of arms to another.

I stepped in front of her and smiled down at the woman who had made my cousins, Brandon and Tyler, so incredibly happy. "Laura, you look absolutely beautiful."

And she did.

Her hair was swept up in a fashion that was both feminine and suited her face. I could see the twin bite marks on her exposed shoulders and suppressed the shifter rumble that passed through me at the sight.

One day Scott and I would mark our mate like that too.

Laura looked up and smiled at them. "Wow, you two look amazing."

I grinned and inclined my head. "Thanks."

My gaze strayed back to where the woman in silver stood eating one of the pastries that adorned the table. I forced my attention back to Laura. It was a struggle, though.

The other woman's pull was magnetic and I clenched my jaw to stop from turning back.

Laura sat up straighter and glanced in the same direction, a puzzled look on her face. "What are you two staring at so intensely?"

She put out a hand and I lifted her off the chair, steadying her as she wobbled.

"Oh, that's better." She adjusted her white dress, which looked like it had some sort of corset thing underneath. It gave her a lovely hourglass shape, but I wasn't sure how comfortable it would be.

"Laura, who is the woman in the silver dress?" Scott asked.

Laura's eyes widened, then she turned and scanned the area while I held my breath. "Oh, she came!"

Laura clapped her hands and took a step in that direction.

Despite me being the athlete, it was Scott who moved first. His hand shot out as quickly as a rattlesnake and stopped her in her tracks. "Is she a friend of yours, Laura?"

Scott's voice was even deeper than usual now. I'd never heard him sound like that before. Scott had always put up a strong front when it came to the subject of our fated mate. He'd been adamant that he wouldn't even want her if she finally did show up, but that was all it was.

A front.

Yes, brother. We've found her. I haven't even touched her, yet I can feel her drawing me in. You can too and I know you're probably terrified, but don't be!

Laura cocked her head and stared at Scott. "She's my cousin from up north. I invited her to my wedding with Tyler but she couldn't come as it was held during the week, so I told her about today and extended the time a little so she'd miss the ceremony itself. Though..." She tapped her foot a little and pulled her arm out of Scott's grip.

"I won't be upset if she knows that I'm mated to both Tyler *and* Brandon. My family will work it out eventually."

Ah, I'd forgotten about that complication. Non-shifters didn't understand the bond that could form between three people like we did.

My stomach flickered and I ground my teeth. Back to the issue at hand.

"Can you introduce us?" I needed to touch Laura's cousin to confirm whether she really was *our woman.* Or not.

But in my heart, I already knew she was mine. And my brother's. She was *ours.*

"Sure..." Laura sashayed through the throng of people and made her way to the woman's side. Scott and I followed in her wake.

Excitement rose within my belly and I was reminded of the year I'd turned fourteen and went on my first date. In fact, I was probably *less* nervous back then.

"You came!" Laura cried as she threw her arms around the woman in silver, who laughed and hugged her back.

Come on, come on.

Laura pulled back and stared at her cousin. "I don't mean to be rude, but you look like shit, Ash."

I frowned at Laura. That wasn't a nice thing to say to her cousin, let alone a woman that beautiful.

My balls tightened as I took my time admiring her voluptuous figure. I usually dated women who were ultra-fit and trained hard to minimize their body fat.

In this moment, I was instantly converted to admiring women with fuller figures. I'd never noticed how incredible bigger breasts could be, or how lush hips should be admired, not exercised into nonexistence.

I'd never look at a woman's body the same way again.

The woman Laura had called *Ash*, sighed. "Thanks, sweetie, I know. Whereas you look bloody fantastic."

Laura did a twirl and stuck her hip out at an angle. Cheeky woman. "Why thank you, darling. The love of a good man...and all that."

Ash quirked an eyebrow at Laura. "Or men, perhaps?"

Laura blushed a pretty pink and stared at her cousin, her mouth tugging down in worry. "Yeah...well..."

Ash, smiled at Laura with genuine warmth and love. "As long as you're happy, honey."

Next to me, Scott shifted from foot to foot, just as impatient as myself to get his hands on Ash.

Laura whirled around, seemingly just remembering that we were standing there waiting. "Oh, Ash, let me introduce you to Brandon and Tyler's cousins. It's common in their family for men to be born into nonidentical twin sets. This is Scott and Jack. Guys, this is my cousin, Ashleigh."

I stepped forward with my brother, my back ramrod straight as I stared at the woman in front of me.

Ashleigh's smiling face turned cold, her mouth pulling down on both sides. "Nice to meet you, gentlemen."

Her tone was like ice, yet I wasn't deterred. Whatever her baggage, we could cope. God knew we had enough of our own.

I stuck my hand out at the same time as Scott. I would have laughed at the comedy of it all if the moment hadn't been so serious for us.

This is it.

With this first touch we would know if Ashleigh was the woman we'd waited twenty-five years for.

She looked at our hands and her nose wrinkled up in distaste, and yet neither of us dropped our arms away.

No fucking way are we backing down, beautiful. Pick one. Touch us.

Finally, Ashleigh sighed and reached up to shake Scott's hand.

Having to watch it happen rather than being the first one to experience it, hit me in the gut.

But even so, I didn't dare blink, in case I missed something.

As Ashleigh's hand connected with Scott's, she gasped and her face reddened.

Then her knees obviously began to weaken as she crumpled and sunk closer to the ground.

I jumped forward to catch her and electricity shot through my body. Tingling pain pulsed straight through my arms and into my core, making my body weak. I almost hit the dirt myself.

I groaned in unison with Ashleigh, as she dropped Scott's hand to cling to me.

I forced all of my strength into my legs and locked my knees while pure pleasure replaced the electrical pain. Like a cleansing white light, it slid through my chest and down my arms and legs.

She's ours.

Ashleigh stared at me from the circle of my arms, her blue eyes shocked and vulnerable. Her lips parted as she took a breath, and I fought the urge to kiss her.

My heart thumped in my chest, and my cock stirred in my suit pants.

Ashleigh began to struggle, her eyebrows lowering as her mouth took on an angry tilt. I reluctantly let go of her solid warmth as soon as I was sure she could stand.

She staggered toward Laura, then grabbed hold of her cousin like a life raft.

My arms still tingled like I'd lifted weights for too long, yet I yearned to have her back and pressed against me. No matter the cost.

"What the fuck was that?" Ash spat the words at us.

I bristled angrily and lifted my hand to signal that everything was okay. Several male cousins around me growled in warning. They could feel the vibrating emotions that threatened to overflow, and no one wanted to shift amongst mixed company.

They didn't need to worry. I was in full control of my mountain lion.

I shared a look with my brother, then stared back at Ashleigh. What was the next step now?

Luckily, Laura distracted our mate. "Ash, how long are you here for?" Laura asked, forcing Ash to stop staring at us like we'd committed some sort of crime.

Which we hadn't!

"Ah... a week or so. I took some leave."

Hell yes!

We had time to convince her that she had to stay.

Laura beamed. "Brilliant. The three of us are going away for the weekend to celebrate the wedding officially, but have longer honeymoon plans for the summer. Will you stay with us next week when we come home again?"

Ash glanced at us for a moment, her brilliant blue eyes troubled.

Then she looked back at Laura, nodding slowly. "Yeah, sure. I'd love to catch up with you. It's been too long."

I cleared my throat and held out my hand to Ashleigh once again. I may as well start the ball rolling. We had the weekend to woo her before Laura returned from her honeymoon, and I didn't want to waste a single moment. "Would you like a tour of the property?"

Ash glared with impressive strength. If she'd been a mountain lion, her fur coat would have been bristling and standing on end. "No bloody way. And keep your hands to yourself."

Ash turned tail in a flurry of silver silk and beautiful brown hair. Her spine was straight as she stomped her way up the steps and into the house.

She's got spunk.

I had to admit I was already proud to call her ours.

Laura giggled, drawing our attention. "You two are going to have your hands full if she's yours."

"She's ours," we said in unison. My voice sounded deep and gravelly, even to my ears. Scott's voice had more pain in it than I'd expected.

But before I could ask Scott what was going on with him, Brandon and Tyler walked up and wrapped their hands around their new bride.

"Hey, Scott, Jack." Brandon's voice pushed into my head and I forced my gaze away from the retreating form of our mate, and back to the hosts.

I nodded mechanically at Brandon, but couldn't stop my attention from straying to the house again.

"Congratulations to you all. Ah...we..." Scott rambled as we began to edge away. I couldn't speak for Scott, but I was pretty sure my twin didn't want our long-awaited fated mate getting too far away either.

Laura laughed at us. "Go, go. You have the weekend with her, then I'll be back and will have her from Monday."

I gave Laura a grateful smile and took off toward the house.

"I can't believe she's really..." Scott's voice drifted off.

I looked at my brother and grinned as we mounted the steps. Pausing on the beautiful back patio, we looked inside the house to see Ashleigh standing with our aunt Rosalie.

"She really is our mate, Scott. Can you believe it? I mean, fucking twenty-five years and we..." I trailed off, a lump rising in my throat when I said the words I never thought I'd utter. "We finally found her."

Scott and I had decided when we were young that the prophecy we'd been told about perfect pairs was bullshit. We'd gone our separate ways, followed our gonads and married women who didn't suit us.

Worse than that, we'd bred with bitches who'd tormented us for twenty years.

Two divorces and five children between us.

Scott cleared his throat with a rough cough. "I...I didn't think she was real."

I nodded and couldn't help the smile that spread across my face. My heart was pumping, my hands were shaking, and a thin film of sweat now covered my brow. "I feel alive, Scott. For the first time in...forever."

Scott nodded and wiped his own brow with a handkerchief. I laughed, something inside my chest opening like a bird spreading its wings.

I jerked my head toward the kitchen. "Let's go."

"Wait!" Scott grabbed my arm with a steel grip, stopping me from going to our woman.

I twisted my arms out of my twin's grip and glared at him. "What's wrong now?"

"Do you think... ah... we should talk to her one at a time? You know... since she's not a shifter. She won't understand about perfect pairs."

I frowned and glanced through the glass patio door. Aunt Rosalie was still engrossed in conversation with Ashleigh. "That's probably a good idea."

I stared at Scott, clenching my teeth and putting some heat into the glare. I was the oldest and Scott got to touch her first. "I'll go in, and we can tag team if need be."

Scott's jaw pulled tight and he huffed through his nostrils, but after a moment he nodded. "Okay, but get your ass out of there as soon as possible!"

I chuckled and turned around, squaring my shoulders as I stared at our woman.

Let the chase begin.

~

Download and read:
https://books2read.com/stalkingtheirmate

www.ingramcontent.com/pod-product-compliance
Lightning Source LLC
Chambersburg PA
CBHW070957190726
48292CB00004B/1487